"He's mine," whispered Lannie Anveill in Meghan's ear.

Meghan heard, but saw only mistily.

She felt, but through many layers.

Neither Meghan nor West moved away from each other. But there was no more heat between them. Their excitement had been iced over. They might have been anesthetized, waiting for some terrible surgery.

The only thing that moved was Lannie's hand, stroking here, touching there.

Lannie covered her victims like a snowdrift with her hatred for one, and her love for the other.

The game of Freeze Tag had gone on.

Lannie was still It.

FREEZE TAG

CAROLINE B.
COONEY

SCHOLASTIC INC.

New York Toronto London Auckland Sydney
Mexico City New Delhi Hong Kong Buenos Aires

No part of this publication may be reproduced in whole or in part, or stored in a retrieval system, or transmitted in any form or by any means, electronic, mechanical, photocopying, recording, or otherwise, without written permission of the publisher. For information regarding permission, write to Scholastic Inc., Attention: Permissions Department, 557 Broadway, New York, NY 10012.

ISBN 0-590-45681-4

12 11 10 9 8 7 6 5 4 3 2 1   3 4 5 6 7 8/0

Printed in the U.S.A.   01

First Scholastic printing, November 1992

Cover illustration by Craig White
Designed by Steve Scott

FREEZE TAG

Prologue

"Suppose," said Lannie dreamily, "that you really could freeze somebody."

The setting sun seemed to shine right through Lannie, as if she were made of colored glass and hung in a window.

Lannie's eyes, as pale as though they had been bleached in the wash, focused on Meghan.

Meghan gulped and looked away, queerly out of breath. If she kept looking into Lannie's eyes, she would come out the other side.

Into what?

What was the other side of Lannie made of?

Meghan shivered, although the evening was still warm. She felt ancient. Not old herself, but as if something in the night had quivered free from an ancient world. Free from ancient rules.

Tonight something would happen.

Meghan stared at her bare arms. A thousand tiny hairs prickled in fear. Even her skin knew.

The sun was going down like a circle of construction paper falling off the bulletin board. No longer the yellow bulb of daytime, it was a sinking orange half circle. Meghan yearned to run toward the sun and catch it before it vanished.

Meghan tried to ignore Lannie. This was not easy. Lannie always stood as close as a sweater, trying to take your share of oxygen.

Lannie stood alone, but Meghan sat on the second step with her best friend, Tuesday, and admired the silhouette of West Trevor as he mowed the lawn.

Meghan adored the Trevor family. They were what families should be. First, the Trevors had had the wisdom to have three children, not just one like her own parents. The Trevors were always a crowd, and Meghan loved a crowd.

Second, the children had wonderful names. Mr. and Mrs. Trevor had not wanted their children to be named Elizabeth or Michael and thus get mixed up with dozens of classmates. Mixing up the Trevor offspring would never happen. There was, thought Meghan, probably no other family on earth with children named West, Tuesday, and Brown.

West Trevor. It sounded like a street, or perhaps a town in Ireland. But West Trevor was the boy on whom, in a few years, all the girls would have crushes. Meghan was slightly ahead of them. She had adored West all her life.

He was mowing around the beginner-bushes. (That's what Mrs. Trevor called them, because they were so young and newly planted they hardly even formed knobs in the grass.) Meghan admired how

West so carefully overlapped each pass, making sure no blade of grass would escape untrimmed.

"Suppose," said Lannie dreamily, "that *I* could freeze somebody."

Meghan could just see Lannie opening a refrigerator, stuffing a classmate in to freeze, and walking off. Just thinking about it chilled Meghan. Even as Lannie talked, Meghan's joints seemed to harden like a pond surface turning to ice.

Meghan hated it when Lannie joined the neighborhood games.

The houses on Dark Fern Lane were new, but the families were old-fashioned. The lawns ran into each other, the kitchen doors were always open, and the children used each other's refrigerators and bathrooms.

Since the houses were so small, and everybody had a little brother or sister who was cranky, or needed a diaper change, or wanted to be carried piggyback, the older children on Dark Fern Lane stayed outside whenever they could.

Even though the Trevors' front steps were exactly like everybody else's front steps, this was where the children gathered. Mrs. Trevor was generous with after-supper Popsicles, and the Trevors had a basketball hoop on the garage where everybody learned to dunk and dribble.

West's little brother Brown hurtled out of the house, taking the four cement steps in a single bound. Brown leapt onto the back of the ride-upon mower, shouting horse commands at his big brother. He had a long leather bootlace in his hand that he swung like a lasso, telling West to jump the fence and head for the prairie.

West simply mowed on, ignoring the presence of a screaming five-year-old attached to his back.

Brown began yodeling instead. He had heard this sound on public television and now planned to be a yodeler when he grew up, instead of a policeman. Tuesday yodeled along in harmony. The Trevor family sounded like a deranged wolf pack.

For Meghan, this was yet another Trevor attraction: how close and affectionate they were. Friends, mowing partners, and fellow yodelers.

Meghan knew exactly what would happen next. Tuesday would realize that she was thirsty from all that yodeling. She would get up off the step and go into the house. Several minutes later, she would bring out a tray of pink lemonade and jelly-jar glasses. Her brothers would spot her, and come running. They'd all slurp pink lemonade and listen to the summery sound of ice cubes knocking against glass.

Tuesday would not carry the tray back. That was West's job, along with carrying back all other dishes the Trevor family dirtied. And West would never complain. He accepted dishes as easily as Meghan accepted new shoes.

Whereas in Meghan's family, everybody hated dishes. It was hard to say who hated them most — her father, her mother, or Meghan. Sometimes Meghan thought the only thing the Moores ever said to each other was, "No, it's *your* turn to do dishes."

West and Brown were framed like an old photograph: sunset and small tree, older brother and younger. They were beautiful.

"You want to spend the night, Meghan?" said Tuesday, measuring her sneaker against Meghan's. Tuesday's was larger. The Trevors were a very sturdy family.

Of course Meghan wanted to spend the night. Everybody always wanted to stay at the Trevors'. Mrs. Trevor would throw the sleeping bags down on the playroom floor and let everybody watch Disney videos all night long. She would put brownies in the oven and, just when you were ready to fall asleep, Mrs. Trevor would waltz in with hot rich chocolate treats scooped over with cold melting vanilla ice cream. Meghan sighed with pleasure.

Through the screen door, Tuesday shouted, "Meghan is staying over!" and her mother said, "That's nice, dear."

Meghan's mother would have said, "Not tonight, dear, I have to get up in the morning." Meghan could never understand what getting up in the morning had to do with going to bed at night.

Meghan smiled, in love with every member of the Trevor family.

"I'm spending the night, too, Tuesday," said Lannie. She always kept you informed of her plans.

"No," said Tuesday quickly. "Mother said I could have only one person over."

Lannie knew this for the lie that it was. Her heavy eyelids lifted like cobra hoods. For a long time she said nothing. It was cold and frightening, the way she could stay silent. No other child knew how to stay silent. They were too young.

But Lannie had never seemed young; and as the rest grew up, Lannie never seemed old either.

The fireflies came out. They sparkled in the air.

We're being mean, thought Meghan. We're treating the second step as if it were a private clubhouse.

Meghan wanted to do the right thing, the kind thing, and have Lannie sleep over, too, but Lannie was too scary. Meghan never wanted to be alone in the dark with Lannie Anveill. Lannie never made any noise when she moved. When you thought you were alone, the hair on the back of your neck would move in a tiny hot wind, and it would be Lannie, who had sneaked up close enough to breathe on your spine.

Lannie could creep behind things that hadn't even grown yet. Dark Fern Lane was a made-up name for a new little development. There was hardly even shade, let alone tall deep ferns gathering in damp thickets, behind which a child could hide. Yet Lannie crossed the street and passed through the yards as if behind screens of heavy undergrowth, unseen and unheard.

"I hate you, Meghan Moore," said Lannie.

She meant it.

Meghan had to look away from those terrible eyes, bleached like bones in a desert.

Once Tuesday and Brown announced that they were going to give Lannie sunglasses for a birthday present. They chickened out. But Lannie didn't have a birthday party after all, so it didn't matter.

Dark Fern Lane was where grown-ups bought their "first house." They said that when they entertained. "Of course, this is just our first house." Meghan kept expecting her parents to build a second house in the backyard, but they didn't mean that; they meant they lived on Dark Fern Lane until they could afford something better.

Lannie's parents had a raised ranch house the same size and shape as the rest, but there the similarities ended. Her parents were rarely home. Mr. and Mrs. Anveill did not set up the barbecue in the driveway on summer evenings. They did not have a beer and watch television football on autumn weekends. They did not make snow angels with Lannie in January. And come spring, they did not plant zinnias and zucchini.

They weren't saving up for a second house either. They spent their money on cars.

Each of them drove a Jaguar. Mrs. Anveill's was black while Mr. Anveill's was crimson. They drove very very fast. Nobody else on Dark Fern Lane had a Jaguar. It was not a Jaguar kind of road. The rest of the families had used station wagons that drank gas the way their children drank Kool Aid.

Mrs. Anveill talked to her car, which she addressed as "Jaguar," as if it really were a black panther. She talked much more often to Jaguar than to Lannie.

Lannie was a wispy little girl. Even her hair was wispy. She was skinny as a Popsicle stick and pale as a Kleenex. Meghan felt sorry for Mr. and Mrs. Anveill, having Lannie for a daughter, but she also felt sorry for Lannie, having Mr. and Mrs. Anveill for parents.

The sun fell like a wet plate out of a dishwasher's hand. Meghan half expected to hear the crash, and see the pieces.

But instead, the light vanished.

It was dark, but parents didn't call them in yet. Shadows filled the open spaces and the yards became spooky and deep, and faces you knew like your own were blurry and uncertain.

Lannie's searchlight eyes pierced Meghan. "I hate you," she repeated. The hate grew toward Meghan like purple shadows. It had a temperature. Hate was cold. It touched Meghan on her bare arms and prickled up and down the skin.

Why me? thought Meghan. Tuesday's the one not letting her sleep over.

Again the warm glow of being wanted by a Trevor filled Meghan Moore, and then she understood Lannie's pain. Lannie loved the Trevor family as much as Meghan did. Lannie yearned to be part of that enveloping warmth and silly love and punchy fun. Lannie would never hate Tuesday. She wanted Tuesday. Lannie would hate Meghan because Meghan was the one chosen.

Lannie left the steps, silently crossing the soft grass, walking toward the lawnmower on which West and Brown still rode.

Meghan and Tuesday leaned back against each other, little girls again, and rolled their eyes, and breathed, "Whew!" and "Close one!"

Lannie heard. She looked back, her little white

skirt like a flag in the dusk. Meghan hunched down, as if Lannie might throw things. Tuesday's warmth was at Meghan's back, but Lannie's hate was on her horizon.

"Hello, West," said Lannie. This was unusual. Lannie never bothered with conventions of speech like hello or goodbye.

"Hello, Lannie," said West politely.

"Are you mowing the lawn?" said Lannie.

"No," muttered Meghan, sarcastic because she was afraid. "He's painting the Statue of Liberty."

It was impossible for Lannie to have heard all the way across the yard, but she had.

"You'll be sorry, Meghan Moore," said Lannie Anveill.

Meghan was only nine, but she was old enough to know that she had made a terrible mistake.

You'll be sorry, Meghan Moore.

I am sorry, she telegraphed to Lannie Anveill. I'm sorry, okay?

But she didn't say it out loud.

"Get off of there, Brown," said Lannie sharply to the five year old. "It's my turn."

"Actually, I'm not giving turns," said West mildly. "Sorry, Lannie. But this really isn't safe and — "

"Get off, Brown," said Lannie. Her voice was flat like a table.

Brown got off.

"Stop the mower, West," said Lannie, spreading her voice.

Meghan tucked herself behind the morning glory

9

vines that had climbed to the top of the trellis and were stretching into the sky, looking for more trellis. Their little green tentacles were more alive than a plant should be, as if they were really eye stalks, like some creepy underwater jellyfish.

"Lannie," said West, "it's getting dark and — "

"Take me for a ride," said Lannie in her voice as cold as sleet, "or I will freeze Meghan."

There was a strange silence in the yard: a silence you could hear and feel in spite of the running engine.

They expected West to sigh and shrug and tell Lannie to go on home, but he did not. West obeyed Lannie, and she got on behind him as Brown had.

How could West stand to have Lannie touching him? Her long thin fingers gripping his shoulders like insect legs?

It seemed to Meghan that West and Lannie circled the lawn forever, while hours and seasons passed, and the grass remained uncut and the darkness remained incomplete.

"Stop the mower, West," said Lannie in her flat voice. "I've decided we're going to play Freeze Tag."

Brown fled. He hated Freeze Tag. Too scary. Brown usually decided to watch television instead.

"There aren't enough of us," objected West.

"Stop the mower, West," repeated Lannie. She did not change her voice at all. "I've decided we're going to play Freeze Tag."

West stopped the mower.

"I," said Lannie, "will be It."

"Surprise, surprise," muttered Tuesday, getting up and dusting her shorts.

Meghan loved Freeze Tag.

Whoever was It had to tag everybody. Once you were tagged, you froze into an ice statue, and didn't move a muscle for the remainder of the game. Eventually the whole neighborhood would be frozen in place.

You tried to impress people by freezing in the strangest position. It was best to freeze as if you were still running, with one leg in the air. It was difficult to balance while the rest screamed and ran and tried not to get tagged. But that was the challenge. Another good freeze was half-fallen on the ground, back arched, one arm frozen in a desperate wave. Good freezers didn't even blink.

At some point in the game, Meghan would get to touch West.

Or he would touch her. Meghan yearned to hold West's hand and run with him, but tag was a solo effort.

You ran alone.

You caught alone.

You froze alone.

Meghan tried to cry out, and run away, but no sound came from her throat and no movement entered her legs.

"Brown!" called Lannie.

He came instantly. Lannie's orders pulled like magnets.

11

"I could call my brother all my life and not get him to come," said Tuesday.

Lannie smiled at the three Trevors and the one Moore.

She still had her baby teeth, but her smile was ancient and knowing. Her eyes stretched out ahead of her fingers, which were pre-frozen, like a grocery item.

"Run!" she whispered gleefully.

They stumbled away.

The sky was purple and black, like a great bruise.

"Run!" Lannie shouted.

Meghan could not seem to run. She could only stagger.

Lannie laughed. "Try to get away from me," she said to Meghan. "You never will," she added.

This is not a game, thought Meghan Moore.

Her feet found themselves and ran, while her mind and heart went along for the ride. She kept looking down at those strange bare white sticks pumping frantically over the blackened grass. Those are my legs, she thought.

A queer terror settled over the flat ordinary yard. The children ran as if their lives depended on it.

Nobody screamed. Silence as complete as death invaded Dark Fern Lane.

They ran behind the house. They doubled back over the paved driveway. They tried to keep the parked lawnmower between them and Lannie.

One by one, Lannie froze them all.

She froze Brown first, and easily, because he was so little.

She froze West second, and just as easily as if West had surrendered. As if West, although oldest and strongest, was also weakest.

Tuesday uttered the only scream of the night, as terror-struck as if her throat were being slit.

Lannie touched her, and the scream ended, and Tuesday froze with her mouth open and her face contorted.

Lannie closed in on Meghan, fingers pointed like rows of little daggers.

And yet Meghan slowed down. In some primitive way, like a mouse in the field beneath the shadow of a hawk's talons, she wanted it to be over.

Want what to be over? Meghan thought. My life?

"I won't be rude again!" cried Meghan. "I'm sorry! You can spend the night at the Trevors' instead of me."

Lannie smiled her smile of ice and snow.

Meghan's knees buckled and she went down in front of Lannie like a sacrifice. How real, how cool, how green the grass was. She wanted to embrace it, and lie safely in the arms of the earth, and never look into Lannie's endless eyes again.

Lannie stood for a moment, savoring Meghan's collapse, and then her fingers stabbed Meghan's arm.

Meghan froze.

The air was fat with waiting.
Lannie surveyed her four statues.

None of them moved.

None of them blinked.

None of them tipped.

Lannie chuckled.

She rocked back and forth in her little pink sneakers, admiring her frozen children.

Then she went home.

The soft warmth of evening enveloped Dark Fern Lane. No child shrieked, no engine whined, no dog barked. The air was sweet with the smell of new-mown grass. All was peaceful.

Mrs. Trevor came to the front door and called through the screen. "Game's up! Come on, everybody. One cookie each and then it's home for bed." Mrs. Trevor was accustomed to obedience and did not stay to be sure the children did as they were told; of course they would do as they were told.

But only the fireflies moved in the yard.

Meghan's eyes were frosty.

Her thoughts moved as slowly as glaciers.

As if through window panes tipping forward, Meghan saw Lannie leaving the yard. Lannie was happy. Meghan knew that she had never before seen Lannie Anveill in a state of happiness. Her smile shone on Meghan, as she lay crooked and stiff on the grass.

Time to go in, thought Meghan. Her expression did not change, her muscles did not sag. Her mouth was still twisted in fear, her eyes still wide with desperation.

Time to go in! thought Meghan.

But she was frozen. Time was something she no longer possessed and going in was something she would no longer do.

Lannie stepped down off the curb, contentedly glancing back at the statues of Brown and Tuesday. She headed for her house.

Mrs. Trevor came back to the screened door. "I am getting annoyed," she said, and she sounded it. "Everybody up and get going, please. I'm tired of all these grass-stained shirts. Now move it."

She returned to the interior of the house. The lights and music of the Trevors' living room seemed as distant from the dark yard as Antarctica.

Lannie stood invisibly in her own front yard.

The dark swirled around her and Lannie, too, went dark, her usual ghostly paleness pierced by night as it had been pierced by sun.

After a few minutes, she walked back across the street. Gently as a falling leaf, Lannie brushed the rigid shoulder of West Trevor.

West went limp, hitting the ground mushily, like a dumped bag of birdseed. Then he scrabbled to his feet. He shook himself, doglike, as if his hair were wet.

Meghan wanted to call out to him, but nothing in her moved. When he walked forward, she tried to see where he was going but her eyes would not follow him. Her neck would not turn.

"Come on, Brown," said West to his brother. "Come on, Tues." His voice was trembling.

Brown and Tuesday stayed statues.

"You guys are freezing so well I can't even see you breathe," their brother said. A laugh stuck in his throat.

"They're *not* breathing," explained Lannie.

West sucked in his breath. He stood so still he seemed to have been tagged again. In a way, he was. Lannie had placed him in that tiny space after understanding, and just before panic.

Through the frost over her eyes, Meghan saw Lannie's smile, how slowly she reached forward, savoring her power, being sure that West understood. Then, making a gift to West, Lannie touched first Tuesday and next Brown.

Tuesday whimpered.

Brown moaned, *"Mommy."*

"I froze them," said Lannie softly, as if she were writing West a love letter.

Meghan could see her own hair, sticking away from her head without regard to gravity, carved from ice.

"I can do it whenever I want," said Lannie. She seemed to be waiting for West to give her a prize.

West, Brown, and Tuesday drew together, staring at Lannie. In a queer tight voice, as if he had borrowed it from somebody, West said, "Undo Meghan."

Lannie smiled and shook her head. "I hate Meghan."

Tuesday began to cry.

West knelt beside Meghan, putting his hand on her shoulder, Meghan did not feel it, but there must

16

have been pressure, because she tipped over stiffly. Now her eyes stared at the stems and mulch circle of one of the beginner-bushes.

I will be looking at this the rest of my life, thought Meghan Moore. This is what it's like in a coffin. You stare for all eternity at the wrinkles in the satin lining.

"Meghan?" whispered West.

But Meghan did not speak.

"Lannie," whispered West, "is she dead?"

"No. I froze her. I hate Meghan. She gets everything." Lannie chuckled. "Look at her now. No blinking. No tears. Just eyeballs."

West tried to pick Meghan up. Her elbows did not bend and her ankles did not straighten. "Lannie! Undo Meghan."

"No. It's Freeze Tag," said Lannie. "So I froze her." She turned a strangely anxious smile upon West. "Did you see me do it, West?"

They were too little to understand boy-girl things, and yet they knew Lannie was showing off for West. He was a boy she wanted, and she was a girl flirting with him, the only way she knew how.

And West, though he was only eleven, knew enough to agree. "Yes, I saw you. I was impressed, Lannie," he said carefully.

Lannie was pleased.

West wet his lips. He said even more carefully, "It would really impress me if you undid her."

"I don't feel like it," said Lannie.

Meghan stayed as inflexible as a chair, as cold as marble.

West took a deep breath. "Please, Lannie?" he said.

West, the strongest and oldest on the street, the big brother who could mow lawns, and baby-sit on Saturday nights, had to beg. Brown and Tuesday were both crying now.

"Well . . ." said Lannie.

"Promise her anything," said Tuesday urgently.

The only one who knew that West must not promise Lannie anything was the one who could not speak.

Meghan, alone and cold and still, thought: No, no, no! Don't promise, West. Better to be frozen than to be Lannie's!

The Trevors stood in a row, the three of them as close as blankets on a bed.

"You must always like me best," said Lannie.

"I will always like you best," repeated West.

Lannie smiled her smile of ice and snow.

She touched Meghan's cheek, and Meghan crumpled onto the grass. A normal child, with normal skin, and normal breathing.

"Don't forget your promise, West," said Lannie.

They had been whispering. When the screen door opened so sharply it smacked against the porch railings, the children were badly startled and flew apart like birds at the sound of gunshot.

"I am very angry," said Mrs. Trevor. "You will come in now. West, why is the lawnmower not in the shed? Do you think Freeze Tag comes before responsibility?"

Lannie melted away.

Meghan got up slowly, sweeping the grass cuttings off her shorts and hair.

"Don't tell," whispered Tuesday.

Nobody did tell.
Nobody would have known what to say.
Nobody quite believed it had happened.
They never did talk about it.
Not once.
Yard games went into history, like afterschool television reruns.

When Meghan grew up, and remembered the yard games, her memory seemed to be in black and white, flecked with age. Did we really play outside every night after supper? she asked herself.

Meghan could remember how it felt, as the hot summer night turned cool in the early dark.

She could remember how it looked, when fireflies sparkled in the dusk, begging to be caught in jars.

She could remember how it sounded, the giggles turning to screams and the screams turning to silence.

But they never talked.

Were their memories frozen? Or were their fears hot and still able to burn? Did they believe it had happened? Or did they think it was some neighborhood hysteria, some fabricated baby dream?

Meghan never knew if Tuesday remembered that brief death.

She never knew if West woke in the night, cold with the memory of Lannie's icy fingers.

She never knew if Brown was slow giving up his

thumb-sucking because he remembered.

The only thing she knew for sure was that the neighborhood never played Freeze Tag again.

But Lannie . . .

Lannie played.

Chapter 1

For his seventeenth birthday, West Trevor was given an old Chevy truck. It was badly rusted, but this made West happy. He was taking courses at the auto body shop and would rebuild the exterior himself. The engine ran rough, but West was happy about that, too; he had had two years of small engine repair and, although this was no small engine, he ached to use what knowledge he had, and bring that Chevy truck back to strength.

Over the years, Dark Fern Lane had achieved its name. In the deep backyards near the shallow, slow-moving creek, bracken, ferns, and bittersweet had grown up in impenetrable tangles. Mrs. Trevor would not let West leave the truck in the driveway because it was so repulsive, and there was not room for it in the garage, so he drove it down the grassy hill and parked it at the bottom among the weeds and vines. From his bedroom window he could admire its blue hulk and dream of weekends when he would drive it to the vocational school shop and work on it for lovely grimy greasy hours on end.

Sometimes West just stood on the back steps of the house and stared down into the yard. "You can't even see your truck from here," Brown would point out. But West didn't care about that. He knew it was there.

West liked almost everybody. He was not discriminating. He thought most people were pretty nice. He preferred the company of boys, and next to rebuilding his Chevy, the best part of his life was managing the football team. He wasn't big enough to play, but he was crazy about the sport. Fall of his senior year in high school, therefore, was spent on playing fields or in locker rooms instead of working on his truck.

Football season would be over after Thanksgiving weekend.

West spent a lot of time thinking about what he would do next on his truck. He read and re-read his extensive collection of *Popular Mechanics*, *Popular Science*, and *Car and Driver*. He thought he was the happiest guy in town. He thought his life was perfect and it never occurred to West to change a molecule of his existence.

But something happened.

West Trevor fell in love.

He fell so deeply, completely, and intensely in love that even the truck hardly mattered, and football seemed remote and pointless.

What amazed West most of all was that he fell in love with a girl he had known — and hardly noticed — all his life.

Meghan Moore.

* * *

Meghan Moore, of course, had been planning this moment for years.

Girls always think ahead, and Meghan thought ahead more than most. Meghan had worshipped West since she was eight. I'm fifteen now, thought Meghan. That means I've spent half my life adoring the boy next door.

It seemed perfectly reasonable.

West had grown broad, rather than tall. Meghan was crazy about his shoulders and had spent all last year imagining herself snuggling up against that broad chest.

This year she was doing it.

Sometimes, cuddled up against West, her long thick hair arrayed across him like a veil, Meghan would feel the joy rise up in her chest and throat, and envelop her heart and mind. She would actually weep for love of West Trevor.

Furthermore, West was dizzy with love for her. West could not go down the school hall without detouring to her corner, and waving. (Making, said his brother Brown gloomily, a complete idiot of himself.) West could not have a meal unless he was sitting beside her. West could not be near a telephone without calling her. West could not sleep at night without slipping through the privet hedge that had grown tall and thick between the houses, running in the Moores' back door, and kissing her good night.

The only thing better than having a terrific boy in love with you was having the entire world witness it, and be envious, and soften at the sight.

Meghan was the happiest girl on earth.

Mr. and Mrs. Moore were not sure they liked this situation.

Meghan's interests had previously been confined to music. She was in the marching band, concert band, and jazz ensemble. She played flute and piccolo. Since she planned to be a band teacher when she grew up, she was now studying other instruments as well: trumpet, and the whole noisy range of percussion.

The entire neighborhood had been forced to follow Meghan's musical progress. There were those who hoped Meghan would attend a very distant college. Mr. and Mrs. Moore were tremendously proud of Meghan and were sure she had abilities far beyond teaching high school band. They expected her to be first flutist with the Boston Symphony Orchestra, and cut records, and be on television.

They were not thrilled that West Trevor was cutting into Meghan's practice time. With much difficulty (they had to look out the window or down at the table instead of at their daughter) they gave stern talks on sex, babies, AIDS, and life in general.

Meghan nodded reassuringly, said the things she knew they wanted to hear, and went ahead with her own plans.

Two houses away, the Trevors had other things to worry about than West's love life. Tuesday and Brown, so delightful and compatible as small children, had become extremely difficult teenagers. Mr. and Mrs. Trevor were worrying pretty much full-time about Tuesday and Brown. They could not imagine where they had gone wrong. Tuesday and Brown's being horrible was very gratifying to the rest of Dark Fern Lane, after having had the perfect Trevor family held up in front of them all those elementary school years.

West, at seventeen, with his driver's license and his good grades and his busy life, was their success story.

Still, his mother was not sure she liked the intensity of this relationship with little Meghan Moore. "He's only seventeen," West's mother would say nervously, as if she thought West and Meghan were going to get married when she wasn't looking.

It wasn't marriage that worried West's father. He chose not to say what he had been doing with girls when he was seventeen. He thought it was just as well that the Chevy truck was not in good enough condition to drive farther than the vocational school repair bays. He tried not to laugh when he looked at his son. He had never seen a boy so thoroughly smitten.

Young love, thought West's father, smiling. There's nothing like it.

Meghan herself had everything: two parents who lived together and loved her, neighbors who included her, a boy who worshipped her, and a school in which she was popular and successful.

Meghan did not analyze these things. She did not ask why she was so lucky, nor worry about the people who were not. She was fifteen, which is not a particularly kind age. It's much better than thirteen, of course, and greatly superior to fourteen, but age sixteen is where compassion begins and the heart is moved by the plight of strangers.

Meghan was fifteen and her world was West and West was world enough.

Nobody knew what Lannie Anveill thought.

And nobody cared.

Meghan danced down the hall to West's locker. In the shelter of the ten-inch wide metal door, they kissed. Then they laughed, the self-conscious but wildly happy laugh they shared. Then they held hands and admired each other's beauty.

"I've got Mom's car for the day," said West.

They were airborne with the thought of a front seat together.

Meghan slid the strap of her bookbag over her shoulder. West slid his over his opposite shoulder. They wrapped their arms around each other's waists, and slowly made their way out of the school.

Every girl daydreams of a boy so in love he can't bear spending time away from her. There were a thousand boys in that high school and maybe ten had ever behaved like this. The girls watched West watching Meghan. They ached to be Meghan, to have West, to be adored like that. They saw how his hands and his eyes were all over her. How he was thick in the clouds of his love.

West did not see a single girl except Meghan.

Meghan, of course, saw all the girls, and knew exactly how envious they were, and got an extra jolt of pleasure from it.

Lannie Anveill fell in step with them.

Meghan could not believe it. There were certain rules of etiquette, and one was that you did not join a couple who were linked body and soul. Meghan glared at Lannie to make her go away, and Lannie glared right back. Meghan flinched. She had forgotten the power of Lannie's eyes. They went too deep.

West remembered his manners — he had fine manners; sometimes he stood behind his manners like a safety rail — and said cheerfully, "Hi, Lannie. What's up?"

Lannie stood still. She was still thin and wispy, looking little older than she had when they had played yard games. It was a little spooky, really, the way Lannie did not age. As if she would bypass all that tiresome human stuff of stages and ages. Her bleached-out eyes passed straight through Meghan and came out the other side.

Meghan, lovely in casual plaid wool pants and clinging dark sweater, felt stripped. As if Lannie did not see clothes. Only interior weaknesses.

Lannie discarded Meghan from her sight. She focused on West. Sternness left her. Hostility left her. With unusual softness, Lannie said to him, "It's time."

Meghan felt a strange tremor.

West smiled politely. "Time for what, babe?" He called girls who did not interest him "babe." He did not know how much this annoyed them.

"You remember," said Lannie.

West considered this. One of his nicest traits was

being serious when being serious counted. Not every seventeen-year-old boy had figured out how to do this. "Remember what?" he asked her at last.

"Your promise," said Lannie.

Something cold shivered in Meghan's memory.

West was blank. He said, "Am I taking everybody to a movie or something? Sorry, Lannie, I'm a little off-center today." He pulled Meghan close, to demonstrate what put him off-center. "Remind me, babe."

Lannie tightened like a bow and arrow. "You must remember!" she whispered so hotly she could have lit a match with her breath.

West frowned. "Ummm. Lannie, I'm sorry, I'm not sure what we're talking about."

"Give us a hint," said Meghan. From the lofty position of Us — she had a partner, she had a boyfriend, she was a pair — she could look down on Lannie, who was alone and unloved and unpaired. It was more comfortable to be scornful than to be scared. So Meghan looked down on Lannie, and it showed.

Somewhere from the distant past she heard Lannie say, *"You'll be sorry, Meghan Moore."* Something in Meghan Moore quivered like a rabbit as the fox's jaws close on its leg.

"You want a reminder, Meghan Moore?" said Lannie Anveill. "Fine. Tomorrow. You will be reminded."

Meghan's knees were weak. She could remember that, too. That moment when her body failed her.

Lannie turned and walked away, vanishing in the

high school crowds with the same ease she used to vanish on Dark Fern Lane.

Meghan forced a giggle. When she took West's hand, hers was sweaty. *I always hated it when Lannie joined the neighborhood,* thought Meghan. *The last thing I want her to join is* us. *She has no right.*

West said, "Didn't she sound like the voice of doom?"

Meghan dropped her voice an octave. *"You will be reminded."*

They actually laughed.

Chapter 2

It was a good morning. One of the best.

In geometry Meghan learned the new formula right away and her mind glittered with pleasure. There was nothing like mastering math to make you feel like a genius.

In history, usually so dusty and remote, the teacher read an exciting passage from an old, old journal. Meghan's skin prickled, imagining how it had been back then.

"Why is history important?" said the teacher. His voice was soft, uttering a sentence he wanted the students to carry through life. "Because . . . if you forget history, you are doomed to repeat it."

Where did I just hear that word? thought Meghan. You don't hear it very often. How dark it is. A word for death and eternal sorrow.

"*Doomed*," repeated the teacher softly.

But I have no history, Meghan thought. So I am not doomed to repeat anything.

In Spanish, Meghan was required to read a passage aloud. For the first time ever in foreign language class, her tongue knew how to sound. She felt a wild surge of triumph, and yearned to speak with somebody Spanish.

She could hardly wait for lunch, to tell West.

Sometimes school frightened Meghan. Sometimes she failed, or it failed her. Sometimes it puzzled her or left her behind.

But this was not one of those days.

She burned with excitement. She savored the feel, even the taste of the new Spanish syllables. She planned the phrases she would use to describe the new knowledge.

She danced down the hallway to where they always met, at the drinking fountain.

He was there already, smiling.

Oh, how she loved him! He was West, wide and handsome and fascinating and wonderful, and most of all, *hers*.

For years she had averted her eyes from any boy she liked. All through middle school, the more she liked a boy, the less able she was to look at him.

But she could look at West. Soak him up. Like a flower facing the sun.

He started talking first. "Guess what."

"What?" They saved things for each other; tiny tales of success to hand each other at lunch, and after school, and on the phone.

"We had a quiz in physics. Guess what I got." West was shining.

He wanted to be an engineer and design cars. He loved anything to do with motors or movement. "A hundred," guessed Meghan.

"Yes!" West hugged her with his pride. "I raised the curve," he bragged.

"Yeah, you toad," said another kid from physics. He punched West cheerfully. "I was the next highest," he confided to Meghan. "I got eighty-nine."

"Congratulations," said Meghan. West's hand on her waist was opening and closing, going nowhere and yet exploring. She loved being possessed like that — the proof of his clasp like a bracelet: this is mine, it stays here.

"You want to get in the sandwich line or the hot line?" asked West.

They checked out other people's trays. The hot plate was unrecognizable. It was brown and it had gravy, and that was all you could be sure of.

"Sandwiches," said Meghan.

"Sandwiches," agreed West.

They laughed and wanted to kiss in front of everybody, but didn't. Still, it was in their eyes and in the way they walked.

"Guess what," said Meghan.

"You got a hundred in Spanish."

"We didn't have a quiz. But listen to me talk. I'm going to knock your socks off with my accent."

"I'm ready," said West. He tugged his pant legs up so they could watch when his socks came off. Meghan giggled.

Somebody screamed.

Of course, the cafeteria was always noisy. People yelled, laughed, talked, gossiped, burped, scraped chairs, and dropped dishes. A scream was not extraordinary.

But this was a scream of terror.

It was the kind of scream that grabbed at the roots of your heart, and wrenched the air out of your lungs, and made you want your back against a wall.

Five hundred students went silent, breath caught, looking for the source of the terrible scream. Eyes sped around the room like paired animals, seeking the terror.

Meghan had a queer slicing memory, like a knife, a knife dripping with blood, and somehow it was mixed with Tuesday, and grass, and darkness, and childhood.

The last time I heard a scream like that . . . thought Meghan.

But she could not quite remember the last time she had heard a scream like that.

West sucked in his breath. Her hand was on his back and she felt his ribs and chest expand, and felt them stay expanded, as if holding onto his lungs would keep him alive. As if there were danger of not being alive.

Toppled on the floor, like a statue knocked over by a vandal, was a girl. One leg remained raised and off it, a long skirt hung like drapery.

"She fainted," said somebody.

"Give her air."

"Call an ambulance."

Teachers and cafeteria workers rushed over to help.

The girl was stiff.

"She's . . . sort of . . . frozen," said the cafeteria

monitor, backing away, as if it were a virus, and would leap free of the fallen girl and attack the rest.

People touched the frozen girl with a single extended finger, and then pulled back, afraid, even wiping their hands off on their trousers.

The air swirled around Meghan Moore and West Trevor.

Old air. The air of their childhoods.

Memory.

The quiet of the night came back, and the softness of the summer, and the deepness of the horror.

Meghan remembered the morning glory by the steps, whose bright blue flowers had slid into their green envelopes, saving its glory for dawn. Meghan had always wondered what morning glories knew that people did not.

She remembered the lawnmower and the scent of the cut grass, the setting sun and the thickness of dusk.

She remembered the calm explanatory voice. *It's Freeze Tag. So I froze her.*

"Who is it, does anybody know?" said the teachers.

"Jessica," said somebody else.

The school had at least fifty girls named Jessica. Meghan did not know if this was a Jessica she knew, or a stranger Jessica.

Meghan moved slowly, dizzily, forward. The fallen girl was still and solid. Her skin did not seem tan with summer, but icy blue with winter. Her hair stuck out from her head without regard to gravity, as if carved from ice. Her shoulders did not rise and fall with the filling of lungs.

"She *is* frozen," whispered a horrified adult.

I didn't run fast enough, thought Meghan. *Lannie hated me.*

She remembered Lannie's fingers, burring into her soul. She remembered being frozen. It didn't hurt. And I wasn't afraid, either, thought Meghan. I was just suspended. Perhaps hibernation is like that. Bears survive the winter, don't they? They just turn down the heat until spring.

But a human would not live till spring.

"It must be a seizure," said a teacher, voice trembling. He tried to move her into a sitting position, but the body did not bend. It was sickeningly stiff, as if she had died yesterday and gone into rigor mortis. "Call an ambulance!"

The girl's leg stayed high in the air, like a gymnast's photograph.

West had had to say *please*. West had had to beg.

Lannie had said, *You must always like me best.*

And West repeated like a little boy learning a little lesson, *I will always like you best.*

He never thought of Lannie again, let alone liked her best, Meghan realized. He liked cars best, and football best, and then finally he liked *me* best.

West set the lunch tray down, his face pale, upper lip fringed with sweat. "I remember," he said. His voice was vacant.

Meghan was afraid to look around. What if she met Lannie's eyes? Those terrible bleached eyes could illuminate a dark yard, like headlights of a car. Perhaps Lannie could freeze you with her eyes.

West murmured, "She's over by the windows."

Meghan forced herself to look over by the windows.

Lannie stood alone, her little wispy frame very still. As Meghan had soaked up the sunshine of West's greeting, Lannie soaked up the darkness of Jessica's freezing. Her smile was tender. Her head was tilted to the side, an artist admiring her exhibit.

West mumbled something unintelligible. He shoved both hands deep into his jeans' pockets.

He was separating himself from Meghan, and from the disaster, and even from the future.

Meghan stared at those wrists, at those pockets, and saw a different West: a West who did not want to face this. A West who was going to stand very still and hope it all went away.

She was aware of a deep disappointment in West. His broad shoulders and his fine mind did not match his strength of soul.

It was a thought too terrible to allow. Meghan knocked it away.

Lannie slid between them, materializing as completely and silently as a chemistry experiment. Meghan's body jerked with fear. Lannie was so close, Meghan flinched. Don't touch me!

She gave Lannie another inch and Lannie smiled into the air, but did not bother to look at Meghan. She did not bother with greetings or small talk either. She never had. "We are going out now, West," she said firmly. As if West were a lottery ticket, and Lannie wanted to buy in.

West jammed his hands deeper into the pockets.

"This is your fault, anyway," Lannie said. "You should have discussed this last night, after I talked to you. I warned you this would happen."

Meghan was afraid, and fear made her stupid, and stupidity made her rude. "Lannie," she said sharply, "we had better things to talk about than you."

In the short space of time before Lannie retaliated, Meghan saw that Lannie actually experienced emotion. It had hurt Lannie's feelings that West and Meghan had not talked about her last night. Lannie looked up at West with a kind of grief and sorrow.

Lannie knew nothing of love. Yet she ached for it; all the world ached for love. Somehow Lannie could not understand why she couldn't just take West and walk off with him. Sort of like shoplifting a lipstick.

In the distance came the peculiar rise and fall of an ambulance siren, as harsh and upsetting as chalk on a blackboard.

"Lannie," said Meghan, "undo her. Jessica didn't do anything to you."

The revolving lights on top of the ambulance cast on-and-off rainbows through the slanted cafeteria windows. When a backboard was slid under Jessica, the body remained stiff and splayed.

"Get out of here, Meghan," said Lannie calmly. "West is mine now."

She's in love with him, thought Meghan. She always has been. How could I have forgotten that? We marched our love up and down Dark Fern Lane, showing off for the world. We forgot that Lannie is part of our world. "You can't do that to Jessica," said Meghan softly. "Undo her."

"It isn't a true demonstration if I undo her," said Lannie. "You would relax. You must never relax around me, Meghan. Now go away. West is mine."

"Lannie," hissed West, "what did Jessica do to deserve that?"

"She didn't do anything."

"You can't go around freezing people!" said West.

"Of course I can," said Lannie, with the annoyed air of one having to point out the obvious. "Now if this was not enough for you, I'll do another."

"No!"

"Actually," said Lannie, "I could freeze lots of people. They would close the school down. They would think they had a weird epidemic."

"I would tell them what you were doing," said West.

Lannie put her thin little arm around his big waist. She hugged him affectionately. "Would they believe it?" she said, smiling.

Across the silent frightened room a teacher said, "It must be some kind of virus. One of those new diseases. Like Legionnaire's Disease."

"Unfreeze her, Lannie!" hissed Meghan.

"No. Come on, West. We're eating together."

West actually took a step with her. Actually picked up the lunch tray on which his and Meghan's sandwiches lay.

"Let's talk about this," said Meghan quickly.

"There's nothing to talk about. West promised to like me forever, and forever is here."

Forever is here.

The words strapped Meghan down. Lannie would have West for eternity, while Meghan would go to school alone and grow up and move away.

"Actually I think I promised to like you best," said West.

"That, too," said Lannie happily.

"Undo Jessica!" shouted Meghan.

The cafeteria turned to stare in their direction.

Lannie shook her head gently, disassociating herself and West from Meghan's crazy behavior.

"You're a virus, Lannie," said Meghan.

Lannie had had enough of her. "And you're frozen, Meghan," said Lannie, reaching out.

Chapter 3

West jerked Lannie backward. Her finger missed Meghan by a molecule's width. Lannie's hand trembled, stuck out into the air, touching nothing. The finger pointed evilly on, as if it could freeze by invisible waves. But it could not. Meghan could move and breathe.

Not easily. Fear tightened her up. Her stomach was cinched in, her ribs were rigid, her ankles were stiff. Meghan managed a single half step away. It was not enough. A river between them would not have been enough.

She was going to freeze me! thought Meghan. She was tired of me and that was the answer.

After a long time, she wrenched her eyes off that shivering fingertip — was it shivering because it delivered a freeze? shivering because it was still straining forward? — and looked at West.

How large West was, how slight Lannie looked against him. She was as insubstantial as a tissue, and yet he had to struggle to hold her. West seemed both stunned and certain. Of what was he certain?

Meghan did not know. She was certain of nothing now. She did not see if she could ever be certain again.

What weapon was this — this threat Lannie could carry out?

How would any of them behave normally ever again, when that finger could . . .

"I like you best, Lannie," said West. His voice was calm. It was even friendly. It did not sound like a lie. Anybody listening would have thought that West Trevor did, indeed, like Lannie best.

Meghan was no longer stiff with fear but limp with shock. Was West acting? If so, he was a brilliant actor. Or was he impressed? Memory returned to Meghan Moore. *I'm impressed, Lannie*, he had said that evening on the grass.

Power is impressive, she thought. But he has to like me best!

"We'll have lunch over by the windows, Lannie," said West in his firm adult voice. "And on our way over, Lannie," he said, giving an order, sounding like a parent, "you'll brush against Jessica. It'll count. It'll undo it. The ambulance won't have to take her. Right?"

Lannie pulled her lips together in a little girl's pout.

How strange she looked. A moment ago Lannie had been as ancient as evil, as timeless as cruelty. Now she was a little girl, lip stuck out because she had to do something she didn't feel like doing.

"I mean it, Lannie," said West. "I can't hang out with you if you're going to freeze people."

Meghan suppressed an hysterical desire to laugh.

"Okay, fine," said Lannie irritably. She snuggled herself up against West and walked so close to him she might have been standing on his shoes to walk, the way Brown used to love to do with his big brother when he was about three.

It was good that everybody in the cafeteria was so absorbed by Jessica's condition. Nobody saw the amazing combination of Lannie and West.

Actually, thought Meghan, a combination of Lannie and anyone at all would be amazing. She's always alone. Everybody's afraid of her.

Meghan's hair prickled.

Why? Why were they afraid? What experiences had other people in here had with Lannie Anveill? What had happened off Dark Fern Lane?

Meghan closed her eyes, blotting out her imagination, and in those few brief moments, West and Lannie brushed by the stretcher just as it was sliding out the cafeteria door and toward the waiting, open ambulance.

Jessica tried to sit up on the swaying stretcher, miraculously regaining consciousness and muscle.

"Oh, thank God!" cried the teachers.

Lannie smiled, accepting this description of herself.

Lannie and West really did sit together for lunch. They even talked, and faced each other, and handed each other napkins. West actually seemed to listen to Lannie, and when it was his turn, he seemed to be telling her important things, things worth focusing on.

Meghan could not seem to function. She could not figure out whether to sit alone, or find an old friend, or hide in the girls' room, or go back to class early.

My perfect day, thought Meghan Moore. My wonderful classes, my fluent Spanish, my lovely, lovely West.

Meghan hurt somewhere inside. How could West be so easy about this? How could he saunter across the cafeteria, relax with that terrible hand so close to him — touching him, even?

Was he acting?

Perhaps she froze part of me after all, thought Meghan. I'm not completely here. Part of my mind is ice. Part of my heart is snow.

Eventually lunch period ended.

Eventually Meghan found herself in gym.

She was taking tennis. The school had an indoor court. Never had it been so satisfying to whack a ball. Meghan hurled all her strength into the drills. The coach was thrilled. "Meghan, you're vicious!" said the coach happily. "I love when you play like this! This is winning!"

I will hit Lannie Anveill like this, thought Meghan Moore. I am not giving up West Trevor. And *he* is not giving *me* up, either. She's not allowed to go running around freezing people or scaring me that she might. I won't put up with it.

Meghan smashed a ball down into the opposite court. Whatever had been frozen in her melted. She was all heat. All rage.

All hatred.

Once she had thought hatred was cold. Wrong. Hate boiled in her mind and her heart. The steam of hate rose in her throat. Bubbles of hate raced through her blood.

She could actually *feel* the hate.

She could feel hate take over her body the way Lannie Anveill's evil touch had taken over Jessica's.

Meghan Moore set down her tennis racket. Meghan Moore backed away from the court, away from the shouting coach, away from the beaten opponents.

No.

I refuse.

I will not be filled with hate. I don't like people who are hateful. I like nice people. I am a nice person. I will not hate.

Meghan walked into the girls' locker room early and stood alone among the slick tiles and the stuck lockers.

She let the hate seep out of her. It did not leave quickly or easily. Hate was a lingering thing. It liked ruling the body.

She shook her hands as if shaking water off her fingers. She lifted each foot and shook it. The last little droplets of hate seemed to leave.

I won't beat Lannie with hate, thought Meghan. But I have to beat her with something. So what will it be?

". . . because knowing your opponent will give you an edge," the coach was saying out in the gym. "You must study your opponent's technique. Then you can see the weaknesses and the flaws, and move in on them."

Know your opponent, thought Meghan Moore.

Did Lannie have weaknesses? Did she have flaws?

Meghan would have to get to know Lannie.

There was no other way.

Meghan had a study hall last period. She usually made excellent use of it. Today, as usual, the forty-four minutes were not wasted. She did not doodle or daydream. But she did not study math or literature, either.

She reviewed her knowledge of Lannie Anveill.

Lannie never seemed to get older, or taller, or curvier. She had stayed wispy. Her hair was dry and brittle. It reminded Meghan of herbs that people who had country kitchens were always hanging from their ceilings. There was a dustiness to Lannie, as if she were very old, and had been stored somewhere. Unused.

Or unloved, thought Meghan. Nobody ever had less love.

Meghan's mother used to say that, when she insisted Meghan had to be kind to Lannie. It was blackmail kindness. You could not really feel sorry for Lannie. You were more apt to feel sorry for her parents. There was something in Lannie that precluded sympathy.

Except for the growing of trees and children, Dark Fern Lane had seen few changes when

Meghan was in elementary school. Most of the families who had bought first homes there still owned those first homes.

Lannie's father was the only one on Dark Fern Lane who actually did get a second house. Lannie had been about ten.

Getting a second house, it turned out, was not necessarily good news. For Lannie's father was not going to bring his wife and daughter along to this second house. He was going to live there with his girlfriend, Nance.

Mr. Anveill promised that he would take Lannie one weekend a month. It did not sound like a lot of time to spend with your father, but it sure sounded like a lot of time to spend with Lannie. Meghan had shivered for Nance, who surely did not know what that weekend and that stepdaughter were going to be like.

And when Lannie's mother remarried, too, Meghan shivered for Jason. Jason moved into the house on Dark Fern Lane, and had to live with Lannie all the time.

One Friday, Nance and Mr. Anveill were picking Lannie up for The Weekend, and Nance happened to have a conversation with Meghan's mother, who was raking leaves across the yard and into the street. "I've been reading up on stepparenting," said Nance.

"Oh?" said Mrs. Moore.

"Experts say not to expect to get along for at least two years, let alone feel any love for the stepchild. So I don't expect a thing, and I certainly don't love Lannie, but I wish she would brush her teeth more often."

Lannie was standing there at the time. She had chosen a few pretty orange and yellow maple leaves to admire. But she did not take them inside with her. She crushed them in her hand.

And then there was the day when Jason, waxing his car (he drove a classic Corvette; the former Mrs. Anveill was not interested in men who drove dull cars) talked to Meghan's father. "I don't know how to be a parent," he confided. He seemed to feel this freed him from having to try.

That year, Lannie skipped a grade, catching up to Meghan. Lannie had never seemed especially smart, and many people were surprised that Lannie was skipped up. Meghan understood perfectly. Lannie's scheduled teacher was afraid of her. What better way to breathe easily than to bump up the source of your fear?

Beside her in study hall somebody coughed. Somebody moved his chair. Somebody dropped a book on the floor.

Meghan heard none of it. For she had remembered the dog. She had not thought of that dog in years!

Why didn't I remember? she wondered. Why didn't I add things up? What took me so long?

Jason had brought home an Irish setter. Such a beautiful dog!

Dark red, lean, and graceful.

It bounded across the narrow yard on Dark Fern Lane, whipped around the Jaguar and the Corvette parked in the drive, and rushed back to Jason to lick his hands. Jason, impossibly handsome in his sporty jacket and jaunty cap, knelt to fondle the dog.

How attractive everybody was! The fine strong stepfather! The magnificent cars! The lovely fluid Irish setter! Meghan had been awestruck. Her own family was dowdy and dull.

Jason, laughing happily, had hugged the dog.

"He's never hugged me," said Lannie.

The dog did not yet have a name. Lannie's mother came out and she too admired the beautiful dog. "We need a name for it," said Lannie's mother with great concentration. "It must be a perfect name."

"For a perfect dog," agreed Jason.

They hugged each other, and leaned against each other, as if they and the dog were the family.

As if Lannie did not exist.

The Irish setter, loping over the green grass, passed near the two young girls. Meghan, who was not fond of dogs, shrank back.

But Lannie had put her hand out.

Meghan, in the study hall, clung to the table, sick with dizziness, as if she were about to faint. *I knew*, thought Meghan, *I knew even then*. I knew what was going to happen.

How vividly Meghan remembered Lannie's fingers. Too long for a little girl's hand. Her wrist too narrow, skin too white.

The dog tipped over, as if made of cast iron. It

lay on the ground with its legs sticking out like chair legs.

"Oh, no!" cried Jason. "What's the matter? My beautiful dog!"

Lannie's mother said, "Quick! We'll take the dog to the vet."

They crooned and wept.

They rushed for help.

They showed the paralyzed dog more affection and worry than they had ever shown Lannie.

Lannie's skin was as cold and white as snow, but her eyes, her pale dead eyes, were hot and feverish with pleasure.

Meghan remembered backing away, trying to slip unseen into her house. She had accomplished it easily. Lannie had forgotten Meghan. Lannie's satisfied eyes remained for hours on the place in the grass where the dog's frozen outline was impressed.

The following spring there was another ending in Lannie's life.

People who drive Jaguars as fast as Lannie's mother either lose their driver's license or get killed. With Lannie's mother, it was first one and then the other.

Everybody on Dark Fern Lane felt obligated to go to the funeral.

Only Meghan had refused to attend.

"Darling," said Mrs. Moore, "I know funerals are upsetting, but Lannie is in school with you, and she's your across-the-street neighbor, and you owe it to Lannie to show support."

Why didn't I want to go? thought Meghan, tapping her pencil against the cover of her unopened literature book. The boy next to her stared pointedly until she flushed and stopped tapping.

Meghan tried to remember the funeral.

I didn't go, thought Meghan. I stayed home. Why?

The answer did not come, and yet she felt it there: a piece of knowledge she had chosen to bury when she was young. When she was thirteen. A terrible age. Meghan was very grateful not to be thirteen any longer.

In any event, Lannie, at twelve, had no mother, and so of course went to live with her father and Nance. Nobody on Dark Fern Lane missed Lannie. Meghan breathed deeper and laughed longer with Lannie off the street.

Not a month later, Nance drove into Lannie's old driveway. Lannie was in the front seat with her stepmother.

The weather had turned unseasonably hot, and everybody was outdoors — because nobody on Dark Fern Lane had air conditioning — and therefore everybody saw and everybody heard what happened next.

"Lannie's father," said Nance to Jason, "has deserted us."

Jason said he was sorry to hear that, but he did not know how it involved him.

"Lannie is yours," said Nance, and she drove off faster than Jason could think of an argument.

There was Jason, in his driveway, with Lannie

Anveill. "Well," said Jason. "Well, well, well."

Lannie stayed. Jason continued to lead his own life. Lannie always seemed to have clean clothes and a recent shampoo. But that was all she had.

Absolutely all.

The children on Dark Fern Lane graduated from elementary school, left middle school, and entered high school.

They no longer had neighborhood birthday parties to which Lannie must be invited. They no longer went to the same ballet classes and had to give Lannie rides. They no longer gathered for afternoon snacks at the Trevors', and had to give Lannie a plate of nachos as well.

High school was big and airy and full of strangers. Even when they had attended it for years, it was still full of strangers. Sometimes they went days without running into Lannie.

Even when they saw Lannie, they didn't think of her. They were completely absorbed by their own lives. The whole world, from the President of the United States to their mothers, was remote and bothersome.

Had any of them noticed Lannie?
Even once?

The final bell rang.
Meghan stood up, dazed.
Here's what I know about Lannie Anveill, thought Meghan Moore. Nobody loves her. Nobody ever has.

Chapter 4

And yet, for all that, when Meghan went down the usual hall at the usual time, there was West, in his usual place. And as usual, her heart leaped, her legs danced, and her lips smiled.

"West!" she said.

His smile filled his face. "Meghan."

They hugged at the locker and went arm and arm to the car.

Lannie had fallen away from their thoughts and their lives like a piece of paper dropped to the floor. How remote those hate-filled tennis-ball-smacking minutes became. How meaningless the knowledge of Lannie's loveless life. Meghan forgot again. Only teenagers can forget so completely, so often.

Meghan knew nothing except the joy and the warmth of the boy she adored. Her world was very small, and very full.

"This afternoon I'm going to work on my truck," said West happily. "It's cold out, but the sun will be shining for probably another hour and a half. I'm trying to fix the door handles."

"That's a good project," said Meghan, who thought it was the most boring thing she had ever heard of.

West beamed, and shared his door-handle restoration plans with her. It seemed that both handles had broken off on the inside. "You have to keep a window rolled down in order to get out," he explained. "And I can't be letting it rain and snow inside my truck!"

Considering that it had been raining and snowing inside that rusty old hulk for a decade now, Meghan didn't see why he felt so deeply about it. But she loved him so she said, "I could help."

She knew West didn't really like help when he worked on his truck. In fact, West didn't like company. He liked to be alone with his toolbox and his chore. But she loved him a whole extra lot today, and she wanted to sit on that dumb old front seat and watch him sweat.

"Okay," he said reluctantly.

They threaded through the escaping cars — hundreds of kids leaving school as fast as they could — and found West's mother's car. West measured his happiness by the number of days he was allowed to take the car to school. It wasn't all the time, by any means. It wasn't even half the time.

"How long before the truck is up and going?" said Meghan, meaning, How long before you and I can ride together every day?

"Long time," said West, half gloomy because there was so much to do, and half delighted because there was so much to do.

West got in his side and Meghan opened the door to hers.

Lannie was sitting in the middle of the front seat.

West froze in the act of getting behind the wheel, looking exactly like a statue in Freeze Tag — one leg in, one leg out, half his body on the seat, half still outside the car.

Meghan froze all over again. Her hand froze on the door handle and her face froze in shock, seeing Lannie ensconced in West's mother's car. Meghan's mind and heart and body raced through every emotion of the day: fear, panic, rage, and finally knowledge.

I know she isn't loved, thought Meghan, striving for understanding and decency. But I don't want her to start with West!

And Meghan especially didn't want to see Lannie so pleased with herself.

West evidently decided that good manners would carry the day. West hated not getting along with everybody. It was a character flaw, in Meghan's opinion. You couldn't always be friends with everybody. But West, like the rest of the Trevors, was endlessly polite. It gave them protection; they could stand neatly behind their courtesy.

"Hey, Lannie," said West easily. As if it were quite ordinary to bump into her in his car. As if it meant nothing now, and was not going to mean anything later. "Want a ride home? We'll drop you off."

But it did mean something, Lannie being there in Meghan's place. Meghan could not quite get in the front seat and sit next to Lannie. Not after she had remembered the dog.

West did not look at Meghan. She could not exchange thoughts by eye. What shall I do? thought Meghan, as if her life depended on it. After a moment she got in the backseat by herself.

Lannie smiled victoriously and rested a hand on West's thigh.

Meghan was outraged. That's my place! she thought. Don't you touch him! He's mine!

But she did not say anything.

None of them said anything. Meghan did not think she had ever driven down these roads and kept silent. She did not think she had ever come out of school without a thousand stories and complaints and jokes to tell.

West seemed to sit very casually in the driver's seat, rather like a van driver who'd been giving rides for a hundred years and drove with a single fingertip, a slouch, and a shrug.

They reached Dark Fern Lane without having uttered a word. And it was Lannie, taking control, who spoke first. "Drop Meghan off," said Lannie. Her voice was as cold as January.

Meghan pressed back against the upholstery. Lannie seemed to have lowered the temperature in the whole car, just by speaking. As if her breath carried frost with it.

"Aw, come on, Lannie," said West. "I had lunch with you." As if that were enough. As if Lannie Anveill would settle for that. "Meghan and I have plans." As if Lannie cared. As if Lannie were going to allow those plans to be executed.

Outside was very January. Cold and waiting, the weather hiding behind a gray sky, waiting to blast them out of their safe houses. The ground hard as iron, expecting snow, needing snow.

In the backseat, Meghan felt queerly numb. She lifted her hands, to be sure she still had them. Drop me off, she thought. Off what? A cliff?

And suddenly she knew.

A glaze frosted her eyes, like the day she had been frozen in the yard.

A glaze of knowledge.

Lannie turned around to glare at Meghan for taking so long. Her hooded eyelids lifted and the dark irises glowed like the Northern Lights. "Get out of the car, Meghan," said Lannie, in a voice as flat as a table.

"Lannie," breathed Meghan. She was trembling so hard she did not see how she could pick up her bookbag, or find the door handle.

Lannie smiled her smile of ice and snow.

"Did you freeze your own mother?" said Meghan. "Is that why the car crashed? Because she was frozen?"

Because that's why I didn't go to the funeral, thought Meghan. I remember it now. I was sure Lannie made her mother pay for loving the dog more.

The bleached eyes swung from Meghan to West.

West's big hands tightened on the steering wheel.

"Look at me, West," whispered Lannie.

"Don't look at her," said Meghan. But Meghan couldn't look away. Nor could she move. She was afraid to lean forward and so much as rest her hand on West's shoulder. She was afraid to touch the door handle, for fear that Lannie had infected it, and it would be a carrier, as wires carry electricity.

"Is that why the car crashed?" said West. His voice, too, was flat. But his throat gave him away. It gagged.

Lannie's smile was as sharp as a splinter. "Maybe," she said. And then she laughed, and the laugh pierced Meghan's skin and hurt.

A few houses down Dark Fern Lane, the school bus stopped.

Children poured out.

Tuesday, who had a generous and romantic nature, and therefore usually let West and Meghan ride home by themselves, got off last. She separated from the little ones. Her dark blonde hair bounced against her neon pink windbreaker. She swung her yellow bookbag in a circle and jumped successfully over an ice-crusted puddle in a driveway. She was laughing. She must have had a great day, or a funny ride home, because even though she was on her own now, the laugh was still carrying her.

"Why, it's Tuesday," said Lannie sweetly. "Dear Tuesday. I've never liked her either, really. Wouldn't it be unfortunate if . . ." Lannie smiled. Then she said once more, "Get out of the car, Meghan."

Tuesday hurled her bookbag toward her own

front steps — missing by a hundred yards — and headed toward her brother and her best friend. "Hi, Meggie-Megs!" shouted Tuesday.

It was a very old nickname.

Meghan hardly knew which person it meant: she felt at least a century older than the little girl who had once been called Meggie-Megs by the neighborhood.

The only sound inside the car was the sound of West trying to swallow and not managing.

For a moment Meghan was furious with West. What was the matter with him? What did he think those big wide shoulders were for? They were for taking control and throwing people like Lannie Anveill out into the street.

But muscles meant nothing.

Not against a touch like Lannie Anveill's.

West's and Meghan's eyes met. This time the message they exchanged was very clear. They were trapped. "You better get out of the car," said West, his eyes going helplessly to his little sister.

Meghan got out slowly, holding the door open, as if nothing more could happen until the door was closed: The car could not leave, Lannie could not have him, nobody could be frozen, all was well, as long as she held the door open.

"Get out," said Lannie, "or I'll freeze Tuesday."

Meghan slammed the door. She ran forward to deflect Tuesday from her path toward the car.

Lannie shifted her insubstantial weight closer to the driver. She said something. Her tongue flickered when she spoke. Snakelike.

West drove away.

"West is going somewhere with Lannie?" Tuesday said. "What is he — a mental case? Nobody goes anywhere with Lannie."

"Lannie needs to talk," said Meghan. This was an accepted teenage reason for doing anything: if people needed to talk, you needed to listen.

"Lannie?" said Tuesday skeptically. "Talk? Right. Lannie doesn't *do* talk, Meggie-Megs, you know that."

Meghan changed the subject. "You're pretty bouncy, Tues. What happened today?"

"Well!" said Tuesday, beaming. "You'll never guess!"

"Tell me," said Meghan, linking arms with her.

What would West and Lannie do on this afternoon? Where would West drive? What would Lannie want from him? Meghan tried to imagine what it would be like for West, sitting in that front seat, Lannie inches away, with her contented chuckle and her pencil-thin arms and her terrible touch.

But from the way Lannie had moved, she was no longer inches away. She was there.

The emotions ripped through her all over again: the fear, the panic, the rage . . . and even a very little bit of the understanding.

Meghan followed Tuesday into the Trevors' house. There was always a lot of food at the Trevors'. Nobody ever dieted there. There was chocolate cake and rocky road ice cream and mint candy and cheese popcorn and onion bagels and sliced strawberries. Meghan's family had things like diet Coke and celery sticks.

The kitchen was entirely white: Mrs. Trevor had redone it a few years ago and it reminded Meghan of a hospital room. It looked like the kind of room you'd hose down after the autopsy.

But the family left debris everywhere: on the counter were a bright plaid bowling ball bag, a pile of trumpet music, a stack of old homework papers, a folder of phone numbers, two pairs of sneakers, folded laundry, and breakfast dishes piled with toast crusts.

It was so real.

So ordinary.

So comforting.

Meghan knew right away that her worries were false and exaggerated.

Nobody freezes anybody, thought Meghan. I can't believe that West and I let ourselves fall for Lannie's silliness. No wonder she was laughing at us. We fell for her dumb story. Poor old Lannie needs to be the center of attention and did she accomplish it this time! I'm such a jerk.

Meghan helped herself to a handful of cheese popcorn and then a dozen chocolate chips from the bag — nobody ever got around to making cookies in this family; they just ate the chips straight — and then a glass of raspberry ginger ale and finally some of the strawberries. Tuesday meanwhile had strawberries on Cheerios with lots of milk, tossing in a few chocolate chips for variety. For quite a while there was no sound but the contented intake of really good snacks.

"They chose me to hostess the JV cheerleaders' slumber party!" said Tuesday, sighing with the joy and the honor. "It's going to be here, Meggie-Megs! Isn't that wonderful? They want to have it at my house."

It did not necessarily indicate that Tuesday had become the most popular girl on earth. Mrs. Trevor was probably just the only parent willing to have a dozen screaming ninth- and tenth-grade girls overnight. Plus Mrs. Trevor would certainly have the most food and be the most liberal about what movies they could rent.

But Tuesday didn't see it that way. Nobody ever sees popularity that way. And Lannie probably didn't see that she had blackmailed West into driving away with her; Lannie probably thought she was just getting her fair share of popularity at last.

At that moment, Mrs. Trevor came home. She was a very attractive woman. Heavy, but the kind of heavy where you would never want her to lose weight: she was perfect the way she was. All the neighborhood children called her Mom even though everybody but Lannie had a mom of their own. "Hi, Mom," said Tuesday happily.

"Hi, Mom," said Meghan.

Mrs. Trevor hugged and kissed and made sure everybody had had enough to eat. Then she made sure she had enough to eat, too. "Tell me that I did not see my son driving around with Lannie Anveill."

"You did not," said Tuesday agreeably.

"Yes, I did," said her mother. "What's going on?"

"Lannie has a crush on West," said Tuesday, "didn't you know that?"

"Of course I knew that. But West is dating Meghan."

"They're just going to talk," said Meghan.

Mrs. Trevor got out her huge coffeemaker, the one that dripped and kept for hours. Meghan was happy. She loved the smell (but hated the taste) of coffee. For a really good kitchen smell, you needed bacon, too. If Meghan told Mrs. Trevor that, Mrs. Trevor would have bacon in that skillet in a second. She would think it was a perfectly good reason to cook some: because Meghan wanted to smell it.

"I feel funny," said Tuesday suddenly.

"You do?" said her mother, all concern. "In what way, darling?"

"Frozen!" said Tuesday. She rubbed at her own skin, trying to warm herself with friction.

There is such a thing, thought Meghan, as being too understanding. Or perhaps that's not it at all. Perhaps I'm just too afraid to think about what's really happening. I'm too eager to put it on the shelf and pretend it's not there. But Lannie's come off the shelf. She's here. She's not going away.

She has West.

She could have Tuesday.

What am I going to do?

Meghan thought of saying: Mom Trevor, Lannie

has evil powers, she can freeze people, she froze me once, she froze the Irish setter, and probably froze her own mother. Now she's threatening to freeze Tuesday. So since we now both want your son West, what do I do? I can't sacrifice Tuesday.

Mrs. Trevor would laugh and say, "No, really, what is going on?"

Meghan was a great fan of television real-life shows. She adored *America's Most Wanted*, and *Cops*, and *Rescue 911*, and all shows of rescue and law and order. She imagined herself calling the police. Hi, my boyfriend is driving around town with this girl who . . .

Right.

When they stopped laughing (and her call would be taped! Her voice would be forever captured on tape — so jealous of her boyfriend she called the police when somebody else sat in his car!) they'd say, "Okay, honey, get a grip on yourself."

"Do you think Lannie is capable of love?" asked Tuesday.

"No," said Mrs. Trevor. She didn't add to that.

Meghan couldn't stand it. She liked long answers. "Why not?" said Meghan.

"She never had any. I've never seen a child so thoroughly abandoned. Why, even when her mother was alive, I never saw anybody pick Lannie up, or kiss her, or hug her. She put herself to bed, nobody ever tucked her in. She ate alone, nobody ever shared a meal with her."

The coffee was made. Mrs. Trevor poured herself

a big mug and added lots of sugar and milk. Meghan thought anything a Trevor did would always be sweet and warm like that.

"Poor Lannie," said Mrs. Trevor. "It's enough to freeze your heart."

Chapter 5

Tuesday and her mother discussed the slumber party. Mrs. Trevor agreed to everything.

Meghan was impressed. Her own mother would be thinking up blockades, barricades. Battening down the hatches of the house to protect the Moores against the cheerleader invasion. Her own mother would confine the girls to the yard and the basement playroom. On the night of the party, Meghan's mother would constantly roam the place, keeping an eye on things and maintaining standards.

Mrs. Trevor didn't have any to maintain, which streamlined the whole event.

Meghan wished she was a JV cheerleader and could come.

But she was not and, as the afternoon passed, she felt more and more left out of the celebration. When eventually Meghan slipped out and headed home, Tuesday and Mrs. Trevor scarcely noticed.

When Meghan was little, the front yards on Dark Fern Lane had seemed like vast stretches of green grass. When they played yard games, what great distances their little legs had had to pump! When Lannie was It, what terrifying expanses of empty space Meghan had been forced to flee over.

Now the beginner bushes were fat and sprawling. Meghan's father liked to prune and trim his bushes, and in the Moores' yard, the bushes were neat and round, like plums. But the Trevors never trimmed, and the long thin tentacles of forsythia bushes arced through the darkness. Icy fronds touched Meghan's face and twisted cords grabbed her waist.

Lannie's fingers in winter.

Meghan sobbed dry tears, tottering among the obstacles.

A raised ranch house has three doors: front door atop many steps, back kitchen door opening onto a high deck, and a door into the garage. If you go in by the garage, you must ease your body between the silent cars and the debris stacked along garage walls. There is an oily waiting stink in a garage. The darkness that has collected over the years lies in pools, sucking your feet.

In winter, the garage door was always dark.

Meghan hated the garage door. But if she went in the front, she would be exposed to Lannie's view. If Lannie was home. If Lannie was looking away from West.

And she could not go in the kitchen door, because it was latched as well as locked.

The door in the garage opened with a raspy scream.

It wasn't the door, thought Meghan. It was me.

Would Lannie have frozen Tuesday? Had Lannie frozen her own mother? It had seemed silly when she was surrounded by the warmth of Mrs. Trevor. Now, in the oily dark, it seemed so very real.

Meghan did not feel frozen this time, but suffocated. The oil that had leaked out of the cars and soaked into the cement floor came through the soles of her shoes and crawled up her veins and lay like a sheet of rubber over her lungs.

West and Lannie. Hours now. Alone together.

She got out of the garage, up the stairs, into the safer more open dark of the living parts of the house. She turned on no lights. She did not want Lannie Anveill, across the street, to see that she was home.

Although of course Lannie always knew.

And Lannie, who could materialize anywhere, anytime, Lannie might suddenly be leaning against the wallpaper right here in this room, with her little chuckle of ice and snow.

It was a matter of will not to turn on the lights and make sure that the corners were empty. Lannie isn't here, Meghan told herself. I'm not going to be a baby and panic.

She sat in the dining room, which the Moores never used; it was just wasted space with a table and chairs. But it had a window view of West's driveway. She wanted to see him come home.

He didn't get home till supper.

He parked that car of his mother's and sat quietly for several moments behind the wheel before he opened the door and got out. What was he thinking about?

He had been alone with Lannie Anveill for three hours.

What had they done in that three hours? West . . . with his Trevor need to be courteous. Just how courteous had West been? What on earth had they talked about?

That hand on the pants leg of West's jeans. Lannie's hand. Thin and white like a peeled stick. What had that touch been like?

Had West shivered and felt sick?

Or could Lannie's hands, which froze bodies and hearts, make other changes, too?

West did not look over at Meghan's house. He did not look at his own, either. He got out of the car so slowly he looked damaged. He had to pull himself along, as if his limbs were a separate weight. He had trouble opening his front door, and trouble closing it when he was inside.

But then the door closed, and he was as lost to her as he had been driving around with Lannie.

The dining room curtains had been put up years ago and their positions rarely changed. They hung stiffly at each side of the sills, as frozen into place as if Lannie had touched them. It was utterly silent in Meghan's house. She had not turned on the television or the radio for company. Her parents were not yet home.

Meghan was so lonely she wanted to run over to the Trevors. Not even waste time getting to the door. Leap straight through the window.

But Lannie would be watching. Lannie always

watched. It was what she had done her whole life: stand in the shadows and watch.

Standing in her own shadows, watching the passing of others, Meghan thought — Life? This is not life. This is a warehouse.

Lannie had just been stored, all these years. Born and then stuck on a shelf, while others lived.

It was time to turn on the lights and go back to living herself. Meghan left the dining room, and walked through the house flipping every light switch. Then she sat by the phone.

It did not ring.

Meghan couldn't believe it. What was the matter with West? He had to know that the most important thing on earth was to call her up and tell her what was going on.

He didn't.

Meghan's parents came home. The routine in the Moore household never varied. Her mother and her father smiled at the sight of her, lightly kissed her forehead or her cheek, and asked how her day had been. How Meghan yearned for the passion at the Trevors' house — the clutter and noise and chaos and exuberance.

"I had a great day," said Meghan. The morning's academic successes might have happened ten centuries ago. "I'm really improving in Spanish. And history was very interesting."

Her parents wanted to hear her improved Spanish accent. They wanted to find out what had been so interesting in history.

But it was West's interest she wanted.

West did not call after supper.

He did not call at all.

At nine-thirty, Meghan gave up the wait and telephoned him herself.

West answered. "Hi, Meghan," he said. There was nothing in his voice.

"Are you alone?"

"No."

"Who's listening?"

"Everybody."

"What happened?"

"Tell you later."

"I have to know now. I can't sleep without knowing!"

West sighed and said nothing.

Meghan said, "I'll meet you at the truck."

They had done this a few times: crept out of their houses, walked silently over the dark backyards down the hedge lines, down the sloping grass, slick with evening frost. Then they'd sit in the front seat of the Chevy to talk. You couldn't slam the doors because it would make a noise the families might hear. Plus now that the handles didn't work from the inside, you didn't dare shut the doors anyway.

The truck interior was not romantic.

In summer, because it was in a low place where vines and tangles grew thickly, there were mosquitoes. In winter, a chill rose off the ground and could not be shaken. Meghan's feet got so cold she couldn't stand it. And this was January. Cold as Lannie's heart.

"Okay," said West finally.

"What time?"

"Same time."

"Eleven?"

"Okay."

"West, I can't tell a thing from your voice. What is going on? Is it okay? What did Lannie do?"

"It's okay," said West.

"I love you," she said to West.

There was a long silence. "Okay," he said at last.

But it was not okay.

Meghan's parents liked to be in bed by a few minutes before eleven, and at eleven, sitting up against the big padded headboard, they would watch the evening news together. In that half hour of broadcasting, Meghan could do anything and her parents would not know.

As soon as their door shut, she slipped downstairs to rummage in the closet, seeking out her heaviest coat.

On the back step, the wind bit her face and cut her skin.

She felt like an explorer on a glacier.

The backyard was long and deep.

There were no stars and no moon.

The wind yanked silently at the young trees and the hovering hedges.

The world swayed and leaned down to scrape her face.

She could not see a thing. But a flashlight would be a diamond point for Lannie to see out *her* bedroom window. Lannie must never know about the tangles, the privacy and the pleasure of the truck deep in the shadows.

How deep the yard was!

I must be taking tiny steps, thought Meghan. I feel as if I've gone so far I've crossed the town line.

The ground became mucky, and her feet quaked in the mire.

Where am I?

A hand grabbed her hair.

She tried to scream, but was too afraid. Her whole chest closed in as if a giant's hand had crushed her like newspaper for a fire.

"You walked right by," whispered West. "Come on. Truck's way back there."

Meghan's knees nearly buckled. "You scared me!" she whispered.

West led her back to the truck, where the driver's door hung open. She was amazed she had not walked smack into it and broken a bone. She climbed in first, and West got in after her, and on the wide single seat they crushed against each other.

"Tell me," said Meghan.

"About what?"

"About Lannie!"

West said nothing.

Meghan was used to the dark now, and could see his eyes. They were large and shiny. "Did you make it clear to her that you and I are going out with each other?"

West was silent for a long time. At last he said, "No."

"West! Why not?"

"Because."

Meghan hated him. Just as much as she loved him, she hated him.

West closed his shiny eyes and Meghan felt buried.

"She was serious," said West. He did not touch Meghan. He ran his hands over the torn dashboard, as gently as if he were stroking velvet. "When we talked, she slid over next to me, Meghan. She never took her eyes off me and she never blinked. I couldn't see down into her eyes. It was like riding around with a store mannequin. People shouldn't have eyes as pale as that. But she's like that all the way through. Too pale. What's human in her got washed out. Bleached away." West linked his hands together and studied them. Perhaps he had had to hold hands with Lannie. Perhaps he had scrubbed them to get the Lannie off. "She'll freeze Tuesday," said West.

"Why Tuesday?" said Meghan. "Why not me?"

West played with the broken door handles. The wind raked through the open cab door and chewed on Meghan's cheeks like rats.

Meghan thought: because West would risk me. He would call her bluff on his neighbor Meghan. But he would never call her bluff on his sister Tuesday. Tuesday matters.

West went in stages with his family. There were times he could hardly bear having a younger sister and brother. There were times he hated their dumb names and wished somebody would adopt them, or send them to boarding school. There were times when he and Tuesday and Brown bickered steadily, hitting each other, throwing things, being obnoxious.

But he loved them.

"Lannie is jealous of us," said West slowly. "We Trevors — our family works. We get along. We talk, we hug, we fight, we have supper, we share, we bicker. It works. We're a close family."

I'm jealous, too, thought Meghan. How weird that I can understand Lannie in that. Meghan thought of Lannie's cold cold eyes growing hot as tropical fever.

"Lannie is alone," said West. "She's always been alone. And she's tired of it. She's chosen me."

There was a strange timbre in West's voice, like an instrument being tuned. *She's chosen me.* Could he be proud? Could he feel singled out for an honor? That Lannie had chosen him?

"She wants an excuse, Meggie-Megs," said West softly. "She's ready to freeze somebody. I can't give her an excuse."

"Just stop her!"

"How?"

The little word sat in the cold night air and waited for an answer.

But there was none.

No parent, no police officer, no principal could prevent Lannie from touching somebody she wanted to touch. No bribe, no gift, no promise could ease Lannie's requirement. She wanted West.

"What about Friday night?" said Meghan at last.

Friday night they were going to a dance. West had never taken a girl to a dance. He'd attended plenty of them, of course. It was something to do. He didn't object to dances as an event. He'd go, and hang out with the boys, and do something dumb like hang off the basketball hoop, and bend it, and get in trouble, and have to pay for repairs.

But he wouldn't dance.

West knew all the top songs. He knew all the good groups. He owned all the best cassettes and CDs.

But he wouldn't dance.

He was a senior, and as far as Meghan was concerned, you could not have a senior year without dances.

There were to be raffles and games and prizes. There was a DJ (nobody wanted a band; they never played the songs right) and the chaperones were somebody else's parents. That was key. A good dance never had your own parents there. There was even a dress code this time: dresses for girls and a shirt tucked in with a tie for boys. Meghan could hardly wait.

"You have to understand," said West Trevor.

He meant he was not taking Meghan to the dance. Meghan could have overturned the truck on top of him. "Lannie won't freeze Tuesday!" shouted Meghan. "She knows you won't go out with her if she freezes your own sister!"

West swallowed. Meghan could hear the swallow. Thick and difficult. "She said she would."

If Meghan cried, West would not comfort her.

He was frozen in his own worries: he had to protect his little sister. That was first with him.

I want to be first! thought Meghan.

She slid away from him, and jerked open the handle on the passenger door. The handle being broken, of course it didn't work. She tried to roll down the window so she could open the door from the outside. That handle didn't work either. She fumbled and muttered instead of storming away. There was nothing worse than a slamming exit — and no door to go out of. Eventually she had to look back at West.

He was laughing.

"You bum," said Meghan. She absolutely hated being laughed at.

West's grief and confusion evaporated. His long crosswise grin split his face. His head tipped back with the laugh he was choking on. He had never been more handsome. "Don't be mad," he said. His hands unzipped her heavy jacket. "So I have to take Lannie to some old dance." His hands tugged at Meghan's thick sweater. "Big deal," said West. He leaned forward, hands and lips exploring. "I'll wear Lannie down somehow," he promised, "and get rid of her. It'll be us again, okay?"

The cold and the wind were forgotten. The torn seat and the broken handles meant nothing. The heat of their bodies left them breathless and desperate.

Yes, yes, it was okay! What was Lannie Anveill, against the strength of true love?

Meghan's adoration for West was so great it

seemed impossible they could survive the pressure; they would explode with loving each other. Her arms encircled his broad chest in the tightest, most satisfying embrace.

More, thought Meghan Moore, more, more, more, more, I will never have enough of you, West. More. More.

A thin white hand ran through West's hair and resettled it gently behind his ear.

The hand was not Meghan's.

A long narrow fingernail traced West's profile and stopped lightly on his lip.

The finger was not Meghan's.

A wrist as bony as a corpse inserted itself gracefully, slowly, between West's face and Meghan's. Fingers like falling snow brushed lightly on Meghan's cheeks.

"He's mine," whispered Lannie Anveill in Meghan's ear.

Meghan heard, but saw only mistily.

She felt, but through many layers.

Neither West nor Meghan moved away from each other. But there was no more heat between them. Their excitement had been iced over. They might have been anesthetized, waiting for some terrible surgery.

The only thing that moved was Lannie's hand, stroking here, touching there.

Lannie covered her victims like a snowdrift with her hatred for one, and her love for the other.

The game of Freeze Tag had gone on.

Lannie was still It.

Chapter 6

Winter wind prowled over Dark Fern Lane.

Snow crept behind shutters and blanketed steps.

Cars left in driveways were rounded white monuments, casting fat meaningless shadows where streetlights touched them.

In the yellow halos beneath the streetlights, snow seemed not to fall, but to hang, separate flakes caught in time. Listening.

Listening to what?

Dark Fern Lane was full of listeners.

Tuesday Trevor was so wide awake it felt like a disease.

Her eyes strained to climb out of their sockets.

Her lungs tried to turn themselves inside out.

Her blood circulated in marathons.

What is the matter with me? thought Tuesday. Her heart revved, and raced, and took corners on two wheels.

After a long time, Tuesday got out of bed. Silently she walked down the narrow hall to the boys' room. The door was cracked, in order that West could slip back in without making noise. Without making noise, Tuesday opened her brothers' door all the way.

West was not back.

Tuesday crossed the dark bedroom without bumping into anything. Since the windows looked out only onto yards and woods, her brothers never pulled the shades down. She looked out their window. Snow was falling. West's footprints in the old snow were covered now. She knew he was in the Chevy but nobody else would. If search parties went out, they would not think of the truck. How long had he been out there? Her heart revved again, fueled by worry.

"Do you think they're all right?" whispered Brown.

Tuesday jumped a foot. She'd been sure he was asleep. She shrugged.

She said, trying to sound knowledgeable, "I guess they're having fun."

"It's awfully cold out to have that much fun," said Brown.

Tuesday and Brown felt weird thinking about their own brother with their own best friend Meghan.

"Gag me with a spoon," said Brown, who hoped that when he was a high school senior he would not disgrace himself like that.

Tuesday had to deep breathe twice in order to say her next sentence out loud. "Lannie's there, too."

Brown sat up. "You saw her light go on?"

"I saw her cross the street."

Brown was full of admiration. Nobody ever saw Lannie cross the street. She just vanished and then reappeared.

"She loves West," said Tuesday.

"She always has. Talk about making me gag. I think we'd have to give West over to terrorists for a hostage if he ever loved Lannie back."

"Lannie's the terrorist," said Tuesday. I am terrorized, thought Tuesday. "Let's go down to the yard and check on them," she said.

"Yeah, but . . . what if . . . West and Meghan . . . you know . . . like . . . ick," said Brown.

What did Lannie have to do with it? Why was Lannie out there in the snow at one in the morning?

"Something happened in school," said Tuesday. How odd her voice sounded. Like somebody else's. She tried to catch her voice and bring it home. "This girl. In the cafeteria. At first everybody thought it was an unexplained paralysis. A girl named Jodie. But then somebody said it was Jennifer, and she had fallen down and broken her spine. And then somebody else was sure it was Jacqueline and she had a fever and some virus attacked her brain and turned her stiff as a board."

"Get to the point," said Brown.

"It was some girl, okay? And Lannie froze her. The way she did that time when we were little and Freeze Tag was real."

"It was never real," said Brown.

"Then why are you pulling the covers back up? It's because you remember that night, Brown."

"Do not."

"Do so." Tuesday looked back out onto the snow. The wind caught and threw it, as if the wind were having a snowball fight with its friends. The backyard tilted downhill, and vanished into the dark. A cliff to the unknown.

Tuesday stared at her little brother. He stared back.

"Okay," said Brown. "Let's go look. But it's going to be tough living with West if it turns out we're just interrupting the good parts."

The door of the truck cab was open.

Lannie was swinging on it, pushing herself back and forth with one small foot. She was smiling as she looked inside.

She knew Tuesday and Brown had joined her but she did not look at them. She was too pleased by the inside of the Chevy.

Brown took Tuesday's hand. She was glad to grip it. They did not let themselves touch Lannie. They peered into the truck.

Two statues. As cold and white as marble.

Carved in a half embrace; lips not quite touching; eyes not quite closed.

Lannie chuckled. "Hello, Tuesday," said Lannie. "Hello, Brown."

The snow ceased to fall. The wind ceased to blow. The world was smooth and pure and white. It lay soft and glittering and glowing on all sides.

"Are they dead?" whispered Brown.

"Just frozen." The chuckle was full of rage.

I have to reason with her, thought Tuesday. I remember that night in the grass. The last time we ever played Freeze Tag. West reasoned with her. He told her he was impressed. "I'm impressed, Lannie," said Tuesday. "They look very real."

Lannie favored Tuesday with a look of disgust. "They are real. They are your brother and your neighbor." She made "neighbor" sound like "road-kill."

"They'll die if they're left out here," said Tuesday.

"If they wanted to stay inside, they should have," said Lannie. "He promised to like me best." Her voice was slight, and yet filling, like a very sweet dessert. "He broke his promise."

Tuesday wet her lips. Mistake. The winter wind penetrated every wrinkle, chapping them. "Let's give West a second chance," said Tuesday. She had to look away from her frozen brother. "He'll keep his promise now." She wondered if West could hear her, deep inside his ice. Could he hear, would he listen, would he obey? It was his life.

"They didn't believe I could do it."

Tuesday suffocated in the sweetness of Lannie's tiny voice. "I believed you," said Tuesday quickly. She smiled, trying to look like an ally, a friend, a person whose brother was worth rescuing.

Brown was not willing to cater to Lannie. "You're a pain, Lannie," he said angrily. "You don't have any right to scare people."

"But people," said Lannie, smiling, "are right to be scared." Her hair was thin and did not lie down flat, but stuck out of her head in dry pale clumps.

"Undo them right this minute," said Brown. "Or I'll go and get my mother and father."

Lannie laughed out loud. "It won't be the first time in history two dumb teenagers froze to death while necking in a stupid place at a stupid time."

"Or call 911," said Brown. "They'll save them."

"No," said Lannie gently. "They can't."

Even Lannie's words could freeze. Tuesday's leaping lungs and throbbing heart went into slow motion, and her skipping mind fell down. No. Rescue teams cannot save them. Our mother and father cannot save them. That terrible little phrase "froze to death" hung in front of all Tuesday's thoughts like an icicle hanging off a porch.

At first Tuesday was going to say, *Brown and I will do anything you want, anything at all, if only you'll undo West and Meghan.* But she thought better of it. What promise would Lannie extract? What kind of terrible corner would Brown and Tuesday be in then?

So she said, "You love him, Lannie. He's better alive. Much more fun."

"He broke his promise."

"But he's learned his lesson now. He's in there now, listening. He's ready, Lannie."

Lannie appeared to consider it. Her eyes shifted from hot to cold like faucets in the shower. "I love doing this," she told Tuesday at last. Her voice was curiously rich.

Rich with what?

Desire, thought Tuesday. Not for West, and yet

it was desire. An unstoppable desire to cause hurt.

The texture of the snow changed.

It became very soft, like an old cozy blanket.

The moon shone through the thin moving clouds, and the snow sparkled in the darkness of night.

The temperature dropped like a falling stone.

She has to undo them! thought Tuesday. What can I offer her? What do I have? My brother! My best friend!

Tuesday scraped through her mind, hunting for anything, the barest scrap, to offer Lannie Anveill.

Lannie swung on the truck door again, making a wide smooth pocket in the snowdrifts. She might have been a six-year-old at a birthday party. Any minute she might lie down in the snow and make an angel.

Lannie. An angel.

Tuesday did not let herself fall into hysteria. She said brightly, "I know, Lannie! You can come to the JV cheerleader slumber party!" Her voice was stacked with false enthusiasm. "At our house! And we'll have a great time."

Lannie stopped swinging. She looked briefly at Tuesday, and briefly into the truck.

"But not Meghan," added Tuesday quickly. "She won't get to come. Only you."

Lannie tilted her head.

"All you have to do is unfreeze them," coaxed Tuesday. She made her voice rich, too. Desire for Lannie's company. Desire to be a friend to Lannie. "And you'll have a boyfriend, a dance, and a party, Lannie. All coming up soon. Won't it be fun?"

Brown was staring at his sister as if they had never met before.

"Well," said Lannie finally.

"Great!" cried Tuesday. "You're going to undo them! You're coming to my party!"

"I'll undo West," said Lannie. "Meghan stays."

Chapter 7

"Only," said West, "if you bring Meghan back, too."

His voice swirled in the dark. It did not seem like a voice at all, but like a wind, a separate wind. A dervish, perhaps.

Meghan lay frozen, stiff against the seats and the dashboard and the broken handles. Snow falling through the open door of the truck rested on her face. She could not feel its touch but she knew its weight. It was drifting around the hollows of her cheeks and eyes. Soon she would not be visible, she would be one with the rest of the blanketed world.

A statue forgotten until spring.

"No," said Lannie. Her voice was no longer rich with hurtful desire. It was a statement voice, a voice for making lists and issuing decrees.

No.

It was a forever "No." A "No" which would not change, which could not be bought, or compromised, or threatened. It was a real "No."

She was not going to undo Meghan Moore.

I am frozen, thought Meghan.

It was queer the way her thoughts could continue, and yet on some level they, too, were frozen. She did not feel great emotion: there was no terrible grief that her young life had stopped short. There was no terrifying worry about whatever was to come — a new life, a death, or simply the still snowy continuance of this condition. There was simply observation and attention.

It's like being a tree, Meghan thought. I'm here. I have my branches. I have my roots. But my sap no longer runs. I weep not. I laugh not. I simply wait. And if the seasons change, I live again, and if the seasons do not, I die.

She was surprised to feel no fear. She had been so fearful of Lannie before. Perhaps fear, too, froze. Or perhaps there had never been anything to be afraid of.

West shook his head. "Then it's off, Lannie."

What's off? thought Meghan. What did I miss, being a tree?

She could see very little now. The snow lay right on her open eyes. There was only a yellow hole in the black of the night. It was the nightlight shining out of Tuesday's bedroom window.

Nightlight, thought Meghan. What a pretty thought. The real night, this night, this night I am going to have forever — it has no lights.

She would be in the dark very soon.

The dark always. The dark completely. The dark forever.

"I don't want Meghan back," explained Lannie. "... her frozen. She's fun to freeze. She knows it's coming, you see. It's much more fun when they see it coming, and they know what's going to happen." Lannie chuckled. "I like it when they get scared and you can see it in their eyes."

Yes, thought Meghan. I was scared enough for her. I screamed loud enough to bring armies, but armies didn't come. The snow soaked up my scream. The snow and West's embrace. I screamed into his chest. I don't know if he screamed or not. We stopped moving so fast.

"Now my mother," continued Lannie, "she didn't know." This was clearly a loss to Lannie. She had wanted her mother to know. Meghan found that she could be even colder, that her heart could still shiver, with the horror of Lannie Anveill.

"And that girl in the cafeteria," said Lannie sorrowfully, "of course she didn't know what was coming either."

The glaze on Meghan's eyes was greater. The snow lay on them and didn't melt. Meghan didn't blink. The yellow nightlight from Tuesday's room up on the slope grew dim and vanished completely.

"But Meghan," Lannie went on contentedly, "she knew. She watched my finger move closer."

Lannie's voice thickened with pleasure. Tuesday whimpered. Meghan wondered how long she would be able to hear. Were her ears going to freeze now, too?

"And closer!" breathed Lannie hotly. "My finger moved only an inch and it moved slowly. Like the blade of a guillotine coming down on her throat.

And Meghan knew what would happen and she was afraid."

Meghan could see nothing at all now, would never see anything again, but she knew that Lannie smiled. She knew the exact shape and texture of that smile. She knew it was the closest Lannie Anveill could come to happiness.

West's voice shook. Meghan loved him for that. She wished that West could know he was still loved. West said, "I will like you best, Lannie." His voice shook even harder. "But not if you leave Meghan out here in the snow."

Lannie sniffed. This noise did not fit the dark and the falling snow and the fear. For Lannie, fear and falling were perfectly normal, and so she sniffed, annoyed, calling West Trevor's bluff.

"And that's that," said West.

Lannie did not undo Meghan. It had been a forever "No." West had simply not understood. Meghan had. She lay quietly under her blanket of snow.

"Come on, Brown," said West. "Come on, Tuesday. School tomorrow. We have to get some sleep."

Meghan heard the snow crunch under their departing feet as West shepherded his younger brother and sister up the hill toward the house.

She heard no voices.

Neither Tuesday nor Brown argued with their brother.

They left her.

They walked on into the warmth and the safety and light.

"I like"

Now the missing emotions came: they slid like a glacier falling off an alp. Meghan fell a great terrible distance into greater fear than she had ever believed existed. She was alone. Only Lannie Anveill stood beside her. She was cold. There was no warmth anywhere. She was lost. There was no rescue in this world.

Meghan's body lacked the capacity to reflect her agonies. She wept, but without tears. She shuddered, but without shaking. She screamed, but without sound.

Her only friends — the only ones who knew — who cared — Tuesday and Brown and West — *they had left her.*

Something besides her flesh froze.

She had fallen, truly fallen, heart and mind and soul and body, into Lannie's clutches.

Lannie had clutched her once, with only one finger, and would never have to clutch her again. Nature would do the rest.

Meghan's soul wept for the ending of her life, for the grief her parents would feel, for all those years she would never have, all those joys and hopes and frustrations she would never taste.

Lannie stomped her little foot in the snow. It made a pathetic little noise in the greatness of the night. "I thought he was bluffing," she said angrily. "I didn't think he'd actually leave you here in the snow, Meghan."

She knows I can hear her, thought Meghan. How does she know that?

She has frozen and tortured others before me.

She will freeze and torture more in the future.

Lannie kicked the snow around, like a little kid sulking in her room.

She doesn't really have much power, thought Meghan. Power is hers just one fingertip at a time, so to speak. West walked away, and he's gone, and she lost her game.

And I — I lost, too.

"Oh, all right," said Lannie. Disagreeably, as if she had been asked to share a small piece of cake. "All right!" she yelled up the hill at West. "Are you listening? I said, all right!"

All right, what? thought Meghan. She was very, very cold. She was not going to have many more thoughts. Or many more minutes. So it didn't really matter.

Lannie poked her in the side. It was a jab, actually, again like a little kid sulking — pinching the other kids because she wasn't getting enough attention.

Meghan's hand was moving. Brushing the snow off her eyes. She was shaking her hair. Struggling to get up. Bumping the narrow confines of the dumb, awful, cold, stupid truck.

Memory sifted away, leaving her with only bits and pieces of what had happened.

What am I doing here? she thought.

January? Meghan looked at her watch. She had to scrape off a crust of ice with her nail. One in the morning? And I'm out playing stupid games in a rusty truck in a snowstorm?

Meghan was so cold she really was frozen. She

was unable to gather herself up. She floundered, but did not manage to accomplish anything.

"Fine, stay there," said Lannie.

Oh, yes. Lannie. Lannie who liked to see them shiver before she froze them. Lannie who liked her victims to know.

Meghan remembered.

And then West's arms were around her. He was sliding her out the door, lifting her in his arms like a baby, warming her with his embrace.

Oh, West! West! You did come back for me! Her lips were very cold, but his were very warm, and when they met she melted a little, and smiled a little, and was safe a little.

You lose, Lannie, thought Meghan.

From the lovely protection of West's arms, from the sweet cradle of his holding her, she looked clearly at Lannie. It was the first time since she had been frozen that she could really see.

Perhaps it was not a good thing to see reality clearly. Reality was frightening. For Lannie Anveill stood very still. And very jealous.

And very close.

And her hand — that hand Meghan had watched descending so slowly — that hand was lifted like a weapon.

Not pointing at Meghan.

Not pointing at West.

But at Tuesday.

Tuesday stood very still, as if she'd met a deadly snake on a forest path. Been trapped by a mad dog. Threatened by a mad bomber.

Perhaps she was.

Perhaps Lannie was all three of those.

Lannie's eyes, bleached of humanity, focused dead and glassy on West. "Well?" she said.

West set Meghan down in the snow. He stepped away from her. "I'm sorry," he said to Lannie.

She did not accept the apology. Her hand remained extended, only half an inch now from Tuesday's bare cheek. And Tuesday knew what was coming. And Tuesday flinched. And Lannie chuckled.

"It was just habit," said West.

Lannie regarded him stonily. "You were going to carry her home."

What made me think that love could conquer evil? thought Meghan. What stupidity persuaded me that because West and I love each other, everything will be all right?

A cracked smile pasted itself on West's face. He was splintered and broken. But this was his baby sister. This was his family.

"You know what I'd like, Lannie?" he said. His smile was in a hundred pieces. But he flirted anyway.

"What?" said Lannie, testing him.

"I'd like to carry *you* home." His smile solidified and became real. He took a step toward Lannie. She lowered her hand. He took another step toward Lannie. She smiled at him. Meghan wanted to gag, but West smiled even more widely.

He picked Lannie up easily. She appeared to weigh nothing.

As if she were not a person at all, thought Meghan, but a husk of one. Stuffed with hay instead of flesh and bone. Perhaps that dry straw hair is her stuffing coming out.

West did not glance at his sister, his brother, or his girlfriend. He carried Lannie diagonally up the sloping backyard, heading toward her house. They both laughed now. What joke could they possibly be sharing?

West waded through a drift that reached his thighs. Lannie dragged her hand through it, leaving trails of long thin fingers.

"Are you okay, Meghan?" whispered Tuesday.

Oh, sure, thought Meghan. Fine. I go through this sort of thing all the time and it never leaves a mark.

And then she thought, If I can laugh at it, maybe I am okay. But will West be okay? What has he just promised? What have we just gotten ourselves into?

Brown, being younger, was on another subject entirely. "Nobody else woke up," marveled Brown, staring at the houses on Dark Fern Lane.

But the parents had never woken up to Lannie. They went on feeling sorry for her, because she had never been loved.

There was a reason for that, thought Meghan Moore. Lannie is not loveable. She is only hateable.

West was a silhouette in the dark, climbing and crunching the snow. Lannie in his arms was a pair of boots sticking out on one side, and wispy hair and dangling scarf on the other.

What is her power? thought Meghan. Did she

always have it? Who gave it to her? What evil force was her real parent?

It gave Meghan some peace to know that Mrs. Anveill, whatever she might have deserved, had at least not known what was coming. It was good that Lannie's mother had driven that Jaguar so fast she did not know she was to be frozen forever.

What was this game of Freeze Tag?

Was it truly *forever*?

Did Lannie have West *forever*?

Could Lannie hold the neighborhood hostage *forever*?

Chapter 8

In the days that followed, Meghan found out how cold it is to be without best friends.

How frozen you are when you are frozen out of love.

West never looked at her. Not once. Perhaps he did not dare. Perhaps Lannie had given an order and he knew the consequences were too terrible. But oh! how Meghan would have liked a phone call. A note. A single sad look across a room. Just so they could say: *yes, it happened; it hurts; we're afraid; we're apart.*

But West did not try to communicate with Meghan. Over and over she told herself: he's protecting me, he knows what Lannie will do if he so much as raises an eyebrow in my direction. But Meghan was not sure. Girls in love are never sure.

Bad as that was, not having a best girlfriend was even worse. For you could always count on your next-door-neighbor girlfriend. You could say anything and everything to each other, and you always did.

Tuesday never looked at Meghan either. She had that party after all: the JV cheerleader slumber party. And Meghan was not part of the preparation, and not part of the afterglow. Meghan was alone.

Tuesday's protecting me, too, Meghan told herself. It's my face Lannie's hand touched: the hand that holds freezing in its palm.

But Meghan Moore did not feel protected. She felt terribly, terribly alone. Abandoned and deserted. Without a friend in the world.

After school, when West had the use of his mother's car, it was Lannie who got in the front seat with him and drove away. It was Lannie who met him at his locker. Sat with him during his lunch. Telephoned him in the evening.

But it was Meghan who was supposed to make explanations to the world. Nobody wanted to walk up to West and say, "What are you doing, are you insane, have you lost your mind?" and nobody would have dreamed of walking up to Lannie.

West's best friend, Richard, who found girls a little unnerving at the best of times and preferred them to stay on their side of the room, actually sought Meghan out. "So what's going on? *Lannie?* Is West crazy?"

Meghan did not know what to say. What explanation was she supposed to give? The real one was too absurd. Nobody would believe it. They would say Meghan was the crazy one. So she said nothing and her eyes filled with tears because she did not know how to gather allies and mount an army against Lannie Anveill.

Richard said, "He was supposed to be restoring his Chevy this winter. I was going to work on it with him. It was bad enough that right after football he started *dating* all the time." This meant Meghan. Richard employed the word "dating" as if West had started selling military secrets to the enemy and should be shot. "But now — Lannie!" said Richard. "She has to be the creepiest person I've ever known in my life."

"I agree," said Meghan glumly.

"But after you?" said Richard, trying to get a grip on this girl thing.

Meghan said nothing.

Richard said, "Well. West and I were supposed to go to the big car graveyard down in Bridgeport, and find parts for his truck. We were going to look for handles so he can repair his, and open the doors from the inside. And Lannie said that didn't interest her, and West said he'd see her tomorrow then, and Lannie said, 'No, you'll see me today,' and West said, 'Fine.' Do you believe that? He didn't even argue with her? He's going to stay with her instead of going to the car graveyard with me?" Richard was scandalized. "At least when he dated you," said Richard, "he also would do normal things."

Meghan managed a real smile.

"What is there to smile about?" said Richard.

But it was impossible to explain.

Then there was Valerie. Valerie was a lovely girl, a junior, the year between Meghan and West. Valerie, too, had always had a crush on West. She was pretty relaxed about it, and teased herself, and asked Meghan for dating details so she could pretend it was herself dating West. Valerie took one look at Lannie on West's arm and said to Meghan, "What is going on here? I mean, I thought at least if he dumped you, he'd take me! But no — he's going out with that pale-faced shrimpette from the zoo."

"Don't let her hear you say that," said Meghan. She looked around fearfully. A girl who would send her mother to a frozen death in a Jaguar would certainly do the same to a Valerie about whom she did not care at all.

"Everybody says that!" cried Valerie. "She is *so* strange."

Meghan nodded.

"What does West see in her?" demanded Valerie. "He took her to Pizza Hut, Meghan! I mean, he was willing to be seen in public with that girl."

Eating off the same pizza wedge. It was enough to make you want to cram it in their faces, thought Meghan.

And then there was Su-Ann. Su-Ann, not Meghan's favorite classmate by any means, said with a snide smile, "Second half of West's senior year, Meghan, and it looks like you're out of the picture. No senior prom for you, huh, babe?"

Meghan said nothing.

"Back to riding the schoolbus like a peasant, huh, babe?" said Su-Ann. "No more rides from the cute boyfriend, huh, babe?"

"Don't call me babe," said Meghan. "Don't call me anything. Get away from me."

"Sure," said Su-Ann easily. "Like the rest of the crowd."

Su-Ann left Meghan alone.

Everybody, it seemed, was leaving Meghan alone. She was so lonely she could have wept all day every day. She wanted to talk to West, and ask what it felt like to be near Lannie like that, and what they were going to do about it. She wanted to talk to Tuesday, and ask what West was like to live with now, and what Mr. and Mrs. Trevor said, and what would happen next?

She wanted to be on a team.

She wanted to fight back.

But how did you fight a Lannie?

If West, who could wrestle and tackle, could not fight, how could Meghan? What was the weapon?

Was there a weapon?

"Hello, darling," said her mother. The kiss they always shared rested gently on Meghan's cheek. "How was your day?"

Meghan could not help it. Her eyes filled with tears.

"Sweetie!" said her mother. "Tell Mommy. What's wrong?"

Mommy. As if she had called her mother Mommy since second grade. "It's West," said Meghan.

"I know. Breaking up is so awful. Has he hurt you? Do you want me to kill him?"

Meghan managed a giggle. "I don't want him killed. I just — "

Just what? Meghan did not even know. Whenever she saw Lannie, she remembered, and she believed, and the frozen horror of the girl sapped Meghan's strength and turned her knees to jelly. But when she was not around Lannie, it was all impossible, and she was embarrassed, and felt stupid and hopeless.

They went down the hall together to the bedroom so her mother could take off her shoes. This was always first priority at the end of a workday. Mrs. Moore kicked off the high heels, wiggled her bare toes in the carpeting and said, "Aaaahhhhhhhhh."

"Why don't you get a job where you can wear sneakers, Mom?"

"I hate sneakers. I love high heels. I love shoes. I love being dressed up. I even love work. It just involves a certain sacrifice, that's all." Her mother kissed her again. "Now tell me everything." They flopped back on the king-sized bed, shoulders and heads hitting the fluffy rank of pillows at the same instant. Staring up at the ceiling, they snuggled their sides together.

Meghan suddenly remembered a thousand snuggles like this.

A thousand days after daycare in which she and her mother had bed-flopped to share heartaches and triumphs.

On cold days they pulled a comforter up over themselves and on hot days they turned the fan straight into their faces, so their hair blew up onto the headboard.

Meghan suddenly remembered the purse her mother used to have when Meghan was little. Oh, it was practically a suitcase. Mrs. Moore practically needed wheels to move it. How many days had her mother reached down into the capacious bottom of that handbag, and made all kinds of excited noises and raised her eyebrows and twitched her lips and said, *"What* do I have in *here?"* while the little Meghan waited, full of anticipation. And each day, a tiny treat: a single chocolate kiss, a package of bright colored paper clips, the monogrammed paper napkin from a restaurant or a giveaway vial of perfume from the department store.

How thrilled Meghan had always been.

When you were little, it only took a little.

But I never wanted to be here, thought Meghan. I always wanted to be over at the Trevors'. What was the matter with me? Home was wonderful. Why was I so sure theirs was more wonderful?

"Mom? Did it ever bother you that I spent so much time at the Trevors'?"

"Oh, yes. It bothered your father more, though. I knew you needed the company. You're very sociable. You like noise and people. There aren't enough of us here, and your father and I are too quiet for you. It used to hurt Daddy's feelings terribly that the instant we finished dinner you'd bolt out the door and go to the Trevors', where things were fun."

"Did it hurt your feelings?"

"In a way. I always wished the neighborhood kids would come here for a change. Sometimes I'd stock up on Popsicles or candy popcorn or jelly doughnuts and hope I'd be the one who got the kids, but I never was."

Meghan had always thought her mother disliked the mess of visitors. She turned on the bed to stare at her mother. They never did this. They seemed to talk most easily staring upward at the ceiling and not at each other. How pretty her own mother was. What a nice profile she had.

Why did I want Mrs. Trevor all this time? thought Meghan, and she was suffused with guilt. She buried herself against her mother's warm hug and they lay softly on the bed without speaking.

After a long time the lump in Meghan's throat went away.

She had told her mother nothing. She had said nothing about the horror of Lannie, and the taking of West, and the freezing of her own flesh. And yet, she was so comforted! Her mother was so solid. So there. So safe.

So *mine*, thought Meghan.

She knew with a stab of understanding that she had been able to spend such huge amounts of time at other people's houses because she had known absolutely that her parents would love her anyway. She had been safe doing anything at all. Safe in love.

And Lannie. . . .

What had Lannie been?

Unsafe.

Without love. Without even a molecule of love.

Unsafe.

If you are not brought up in the safety of love, thought Meghan Moore, you yourself become unsafe. It is unsafe to be near Lannie. She is as dangerous as a collapsing bridge or a caving-in cliff. All because of love.

"Ohmygosh!" said Meghan, remembering things out of nowhere, the way your mind does sometimes, all on its own. "Mom, don't you have a meeting tonight? We haven't even thought about supper! You're late! You haven't even changed yet! Ohmygosh!"

Her mother said. "It's only a meeting. You and I needed a hug. We haven't had a good long hug in ages."

Meghan's eyes filled with tears. Her mother had been there, waiting for this hug, and Meghan hadn't been home.

"It'll be okay in the end, darling," said her mother softly, lips moving against Meghan's hair as she squeezed her daughter. "I'm so sorry you're having trouble with West. I know you've always adored him. I know how it must hurt. But you'll tough it out. You're my strong girl. You'll do the right thing. You'll make it."

Chapter 9

Meghan *was* strong. But to be strong alone — it was hard.

She wanted to be strong together!

After two weeks of being discarded like something you can't even recycle in the garbage, Meghan went over to the Trevors' after school just the way she always had. She had the courage to do this only because she knew that West had his mother's car that day, and she had seen him drive away after school with Lannie, and the car was not back. So only Tuesday would be there, and possibly Brown, if he didn't have sports.

Meghan didn't knock. She had never knocked at the Trevors', just walked in. "Hi, Tues," she said nervously.

Tuesday leaped up from the television. She raced across the room and flung her arms around Meghan. "I'm so glad you're here!"

There. That was the welcome and those were the words. Some of the leftover frozenness in Meghan's lonely heart eased.

"It's been so weird," said Tuesday. "West doesn't talk to anybody. Not me, not Brown, not Mom, not Dad. I guess he uses up all his speech and energy with Lannie and he comes home this drained-out old thing. Sits over his homework without seeing the page, without lifting the pencil. Mom and Dad are beside themselves. You won't believe this, but they think he's lovesick."

"Over Lannie?"

Tuesday nodded. "Over Lannie. Brown and I tried to inch into an explanation that the sick one is Lannie, and the trapped one is West, and the one in danger is you. But you know parents. Even mine. They just got annoyed and stomped around when we reached the Freeze Tag part. West didn't like it either. He wouldn't even back us up. He just looked at his hands and said he didn't know what we were talking about."

Looked at his hands, thought Meghan. Why his own hands? Did Lannie pass it on? Can he do it, too, now? She swallowed, trying to gag down this horrible image. "I didn't even try with my parents," she said. She checked the window. There were no cars approaching. All they needed was for West and Lannie to drive up while she was on the premises.

"West had to take her to the library," said Tuesday.

"She studies?"

"She says so," Tuesday shrugged. "She's attached herself to him like a starfish to a rock."

"How can he stand it?" Meghan could not bear it

that West was managing. Was there something redeemable in Lannie that West had managed to find? If anybody was going to find good things in an evil person, it would be a Trevor. They were big on silver linings.

Mr. Trevor came in. He got out of work at about the same time the kids got out of school, so he was usually home in the afternoons. "Hey there, Meggie-Megs!" he said, much too heartily. "Say! We haven't seen much of you lately. How've you been, kid?"

"Fine," said Meghan, because what other answer could you give a grown-up?

"Sorry you and West sort of split up," muttered Mr. Trevor.

Meghan said nothing.

"They didn't sort of split up," said Tuesday. "Lannie forced herself on West."

Mr. Trevor did not look as if he believed that. Clearly, he believed it took two to tango; if West was dating Lannie, it was because West wanted to date Lannie.

"Lannie stinks," said Tuesday, laying it on the line.

"I'm sorry," said her father, addressing both girls, "that this turn of events has happened, but life is like that when you're young. You fall in love lots of times with lots of different people. So let's not say anything unpleasant about West's girlfriend."

Tuesday threw her arms in the air. "Let's," she

said. "Let's say lots and lots of unpleasant stuff about West's girlfriend. And then let's *do* something unpleasant to West's girlfriend."

Mr. Trevor frowned and left the room.

But Tuesday and Meghan grinned at each other. The grin of conspirators. Allies. Teams. They even winked.

"I'm staying at the Trevors' for supper, Mom," said Meghan into the telephone. "And I'll be studying with Tuesday. I'll be home around ten, okay?"

"That's pretty late for a school night," said her mother. "How about nine?"

Nine. Meghan wasn't sure it was going to be manageable before nine. "Fine," she said to her mother. "I'll be home by nine."

The thought of crossing the open space between the houses after dark was so scary Meghan almost quit right then. She would have Lannie's eyes following her, Lannie's knowledge, Lannie's plans.

"You can crawl across the grass the way they do in desert warfare," suggested Tuesday, giggling. "Belly flat, head down, bullets whizzing through your hair."

For Tuesday it had become fun. An adventure.

But then, Tues wasn't the one who had been frozen in the truck. Tuesday hadn't felt snow piling up on her open eyes. Tuesday hadn't felt the cold passing into her heart, taking her into another world.

Tuesday's pretty bed jutted out into the room, leaving a space between the hanging bedspread and the wall. From the doorway you could not see down into that space. Meghan unrolled the sleeping bag in which she had spent so many nights and lay down, hidden. The afternoon grew dark. Tuesday and her brothers and parents had dinner. They made a lot of noise. None of it was West. Five people for dinner and four talked.

But he would talk tonight.

Mr. and Mrs. Trevor would watch their favorite TV programs and the children would be sent to their desks to do homework.

Well, they would do homework. But it wouldn't be a school assignment.

Meghan stayed beneath the level of the windowsill, just in case Lannie was lurking outside, peeking, staring, thought-policing.

It was eight-fifteen before Tuesday led West into her silent unlit bedroom.

"Sit on the floor," Tuesday said to him, and burst into a spatter of giggles.

"Tues, I'm tired," he said. "I can't play games anymore. Isn't it enough I have to play this endless game with Lannie?"

Meghan crept out from behind the bed.

West stared at her. She held a finger to her lips.

He sagged in a funny way, as if he were being rescued. "Oh, Meghan!" he said, and he said nothing more, but it was enough. He sat down next to her, and Tuesday sat with them, which Meghan regretted, but then, tonight's plan did not call for a kiss. It called for strategy.

"What's going on in here?" hissed Brown.

"Crawl in," whispered Tuesday.

Brown checked out the participants. "War council!" he said delightedly, and dropped down, and crawled. He would make an excellent desert warfare soldier, he had that belly technique down perfectly.

The four of them lay on their stomachs, propping their heads up with their cupped hands.

"What," said Tuesday, "are we going to do?"

"You're asking me?" said West. "You think I've come up with something?"

"Where does Lannie get this power?" said Tuesday. "Maybe we can cut off her source."

West shook his head. "I asked her how she calls it up. I was half thinking *I* could freeze *her*. If I knew how. She said she'd stage a demonstration for me. She said she'd freeze that gym coach I don't like."

"Wonderful," said Brown.

"Exactly. I start yelling 'No, no, no, no, no!' and Lannie says to me, 'Don't worry, West, it's easy, all I have to do is touch him, you won't be involved. I'd do that for you,' she says. Like I'd be happy afterward."

"But Lannie must touch you all the time," said Tuesday. "And you don't freeze."

"She does touch me all the time. But I don't touch her. It's not so bad if I just sit there and let her do what she wants."

It sounded pretty bad to Meghan. But still, Meghan began to enjoy herself. This was nice, this meeting of the best friends, plotting in the dark, hidden by the furniture, safe from the bleached eyes.

"I give Lannie hundreds of excuses for why I can't see her every waking minute," West said. "I use sports, chorus, homework, term papers, weather, baby-sitting, Tuesday, Brown, Mom, Dad, Grandma."

"Grandma?" said Tuesday.

"I said when you're eighty years old and you're stuck in a nursing home five hundred miles away, you want to hear from your oldest grandson. I've written a lot of letters."

Meghan giggled. West's face split into the old familiar grin. Oh, she loved him so much! Okay, they were going to whip this thing. Together they were going to knock Lannie out of commission.

"You should have been here at breakfast this morning," Tuesday told Meghan. "It was so funny. Mom says to West, 'You can have the car, dear.' And West says, 'No thanks Mom,' because the last thing he wants is to be alone with Lannie yet again. And Mom goes — 'There's no such thing as a seventeen-year-old boy who doesn't want the car. Are you sick? Are you taking drugs?' So after we make our way through the no-I'm-not-on-drugs conversation, Mom wants to know the truth about why West doesn't want the car. And the best my stupid old brother can come up with is — it's tough finding a parking space."

"Oh, yeah, Mom believed that," said Brown. Tuesday and Brown burst into gales of laughter. West flushed. Meghan rested her hand on his. It was their only touch. The only touch in so long! He lowered his gaze and seemed to draw comfort from her hand. No doubt it was very different from the one that had been touching him these last weeks.

Tuesday became very businesslike. She did not want this evening to deteriorate into some sort of icky romantic thing. "I think," said Tuesday, "that you've given it enough of a shot, West. Now in the morning, you march up to Lannie and you tell Lannie it's been fun, but it's time for you to move on."

West looked at his sister incredulously. "After what she did to Meghan?"

"It's worth a try," said Tuesday.

West shook his head. "She'll hurt somebody."

"We'll keep our distance."

"She'll run after you."

"Don't be a wimp," said Tuesday sharply. "You have to let Lannie know the score. Otherwise, this could go on forever."

Tuesday made it sound so simple. Meghan tried to believe her. That West could just say, *Hey, Lan, been fun, see ya around, back to normal now, don't hurt anybody, 'kay?*

"Okay," said West, nodding, trying to give himself courage. "You're right. It can't go on forever."

Meghan ate a huge breakfast, having skipped dinner the night before. Her mother was delighted. Mothers always loved seeing you eat breakfast. Even though Meghan had fixed it herself, her mother seemed to feel she could take credit for it.

But she was not so eager to go outside.

For this was the morning. West was to tell Lannie to skip off and leave him alone. Leave them all alone.

To whom was Lannie the most dangerous?

Would she turn on West, for breaking his promise? Would she turn on Meghan, for being the one West still wanted? Would she turn on Tuesday, for being the sister who started things?

This won't work! thought Meghan. He mustn't do it! Lannie isn't going to say, oh, well, it was worth a try, have a nice life without me, West! Lannie's going to attack!

Meghan rushed to the telephone and stabbed at the familiar buttons, to call West, tell him no, no, no, no, no!

She didn't get past the second number.

West, Tuesday, and Brown were already outside. West had his mother's car keys in his hand; was unlocking the doors. Tuesday was getting in front — Lannie's place. Brown was playing Indian and hollering and whooping and generally attracting attention.

Meghan set the phone down gently. She got into her coat. She pulled on her mittens. She tightened her scarf. Perhaps Lannie's touch could not go through clothing. Perhaps wool or goosedown could save Meghan.

Right, she thought. There is no getting away from Lannie.

Meghan came out her front door.

Lannie came out hers.

The Trevor children looked up Dark Fern Lane, and saw them both.

West, Tuesday, Brown, Lannie, and Meghan all knew. This was a test. The game had reached another level. They looked at each other and, even from her front door, Meghan could feel the heat and the cold, the hatred and the love, the fear and the need.

No one else did.

Two houses up, the rest of the Dark Fern Lane children waited for the buses. There were two kindergartners at that stop, two first-graders, no second-graders, one third-grader. Then there was quite an age skip up to Brown. Lannie intended for Brown to be on that bus, not riding in the car with West and herself.

The little children played in the snow.

They pushed each other down and then got up and admired the dents their bottoms had put in the snow. They swung their lunches and bookbags in circles and let go, so the bright colored containers spun out like trajectiles and hit the others lightly. They laughed six-year-old laughs and made six-year-old jokes.

The third-grader showed off, doing a cartwheel.

The littler ones had no idea how to accomplish such a marvelous move, but they tried. They flung their legs up an inch or two and giggled proudly.

Lannie Anveill walked through them. Stringing her fingers along as if she were hanging laundry on a line.

Perhaps she was.

They froze.

The two kindergartners, the two first-graders, the one third-grader. They hung in their positions like statues.

"No," whispered Tuesday, who had started this. "No, please."

Lannie stopped midway between her statues and the Trevors. Directly in front of Meghan's. Meghan might as well have been frozen. She could not move. Could not think.

"Hi, West," said Lannie across the frozen yards.

He did not speak. Perhaps he was as terrified as Meghan.

"Your heart is not in this, West," said Lannie.

He did not move either. Had she frozen him without even touching?

"I want your heart, West," said Lannie.

There was a thick dense silence.

Lannie's smile was tiny and yet tall: her mouth opened up and down, instead of sideways, in a terrifying leer.

The five little children remained frozen in the snow. Perhaps their mothers were not looking out the window. Perhaps their mothers thought it was part of a game.

It was.

But not a game anybody should ever play.

Freeze Tag.

No, please, thought Meghan. Not the little children. Not just because I want to be the one at Pizza Hut with West. Set them free. Let them go.

"Lannie," said West. His head sank down, so that he was looking at his own chest, the front of his own winter jacket. He seemed to lose some of the vertebrae in his backbone, and grow shorter and less strong. His voice scratched. He walked toward Lannie like an old man weighted with stones.

"You have my heart," said West.

Chapter 10

"You know," said Meghan's father, "I haven't seen Jason lately."

Meghan and her mother were going through the movie listings. Once a month the Moore family had Movie Saturday. Driving to the huge, twelve movie theater that had opened a few years ago, they saw one movie at four o'clock, came out dizzy and pleased, went to have hamburgers, french fries, and shakes, and came back for a movie at seven. During the first movie they had candy and during the second movie they had popcorn.

Meghan loved Movie Day. When she watched a movie, she fell into it. It was completely real and completely absorbing. Even a bad movie was good when you saw it on a big screen. Whereas bad movies when you rented them to watch at home were just plain bad movies.

This month was a toughie: They wanted to see everything. "It's better than the months when we don't want to see anything," her mother pointed out.

"I mean, I usually at least see Jason coming and going," said Meghan's father.

Meghan had not been thinking about Lannie for several weeks now. Ever since West had had to go on his knees to beg her to unfreeze the little children at the bus stop, she had decided just not to think about it again. There was nothing she could do. Nothing anybody could do. And as long as Lannie had West, the world was safe.

You have my heart, Lannie, West had said.

Meghan didn't think about that either. It had sounded so true. You could almost see his heart, that day, red and bleeding and beating. As if he carried it over to her and set it down so she could have it.

Lannie had danced back among the children, as light as an elf on top of the snow. Flying past the little ones, she seemed hardly even to touch them. She skimmed along like a swallow in the sky.

But the children fell over in the snow, real again. There was a moment when they were all close to tears. All close to calling, *Mommy! Mommy come and get me! Mommy, something's wrong!*

But the yellow schoolbus had turned the corner, and the children lined up to get on, bickering over who deserved to get on first. Shouting about who would sit with whom. And if they crowded closer to each other for warmth, and if a short, cold memory lay like ice on the backs of their necks, they did not say so out loud.

Nobody had ever said so out loud.

If I'm not thinking about Lannie, thought Meghan, I'm certainly not thinking about Jason.

Meghan tapped on the newspaper column with her bright blue soft-tipped pen. Meghan liked to write in many colors. She liked to underline in vivid yellow. She liked to make lists in black. She liked to address envelopes in red. She liked to take notes in blue. She had written very few letters in her life, but when she considered writing one, she considered writing it in blue, too.

Mrs. Moore said, "This movie is supposed to be a really truly weepy huggy romance. I am in the mood. I want love and loss. I want finders keepers. I want rings and music."

Meghan's vow to herself never to think about it again evaporated, as it did, in fact, nearly every day. Sometimes hundreds of times a day.

I want West, thought Meghan. He is all of those. I am going to a movie with my mother and father to watch an actress pretend to be in love with an actor. A month ago, I was the lover. I was loved.

And now . . .

What was happening now?

"It kind of bothers me," said Meghan's father. He circled the kitchen, wanting his women to listen. Say something. Finish up his thoughts and his sentences for him.

Not me, thought Meghan.

At last Meghan's mother responded to him. "You could go over and check," she pointed out.

But Mr. Moore and Lannie's stepfather were not actually friends. They waved over the pavement. They occasionally met in the driveway when each was polishing his car. Once or twice they had each had a beer in hand on a hot summer day and had stood talking.

Jason never seemed to have a part in the life of Dark Fern Lane.

He drove out or he drove in, but he did not drive among.

In fact, now that Meghan thought about it, what did Jason do?

Mr. Moore left the kitchen, and the long white counter over which his wife and daughter had spread the newspaper. He crossed into the living room, spread back the curtains that lay gauzily over the picture window, tucked the fern fronds out of the way, and looked diagonally across the street at Jason's house.

"There's Lannie," said Mr. Moore. "Meggie-Megs, go find out from Lannie."

Leave the safety of her house?

Walk right up to Lannie Anveill? Who froze children like used clothes for a garage sale?

Get close to Lannie? Who when she was done freezing or unfreezing would set her hand back down? As if it were not attached, but was a purse or a book she was carrying around.

Say to her: *Lannie . . . we haven't seen Jason lately.*

"What do you think could have happened to him?" said her mother lightly.

Meghan could think of one thing, anyway. But her mother was not talking to Meghan. Meghan's fingers tightened. The blue dot beneath her pen spread an amoeba of ink over the movie listings.

"He's probably just out of town," said Mr. Moore.

But Jason's job had never seemed to involve overnight travel. Besides there was Lannie. Would he leave a fourteen-year-old?

Of course, it was Lannie.

It was not as if they were talking about a normal fourteen-year-old.

And yet . . .

"Go ask Lannie, Meghan," said her mother.

Meghan did not move.

"I know you're still upset about West going out with her," said her father, as if this were pretty small of Meghan; an event so minor her father could hardly believe his daughter even *noticed* when her boyfriend dropped her. "But I want you to ask."

Meghan was against part of growing up.

There suddenly were times when she was supposed to do the hard parts, when up till now they had always fallen into her parents' laps. "You ask her," she said.

Her father sighed a little, shrugged slightly, went to his office, and shut the door.

"It certainly isn't very much for your father to ask of you," said her mother sharply. "I think it's rather unpleasant of you to refuse him such a simple request. He's worried about his neighbor and you can't even be bothered to set his mind at rest."

At rest? Since when did Lannie's answers set anybody's mind at rest?

Meghan trudged heavily down the half stairs that divided their raised ranch house in the middle. Most of the families on Dark Fern Lane had replaced the thick hairy carpet that originally covered their stairs. When she was little, Meghan had loved that old orangey-brown carpet, with its loops as thick as an old-fashioned mop. Every house had either orangey-brown or else avocado green. It made even the houses of strangers seem familiar, because you remembered the carpeting so well. The year Meghan was in sixth grade, suddenly no grown-up on Dark Fern Lane could stand the sight of shag. Carpet vans were parked on Dark Fern Lane all the time. Now everybody had sophisticated nubbly champagne wool.

The orange shag had been cozier. Shabby, but comforting.

There was something cold and businesslike about the knots of pale wool.

Plus you had to remember to wipe your feet on the doormat before you came inside, a step everybody had omitted back when they had shag carpeting.

Meghan could not waste much more time worrying over carpet. She went out the front door.

Her father was correct. Lannie was there.

Standing thin and small in her driveway.

Perhaps she was waiting for West to pick her up.

Perhaps West had just dropped her off and she was still thinking about it, staring down at his house, watching him go inside.

Meghan walked slowly across the yard. The last

snow had melted and the temperature had dropped even lower. The ground was hard as pavement, and the frozen grass crunched like breakfast cereal under her shoes.

It was difficult to imagine herself and the Trevor children young enough and carefree enough to play yard games here. It seemed decades ago, a topic for history class.

It was me, thought Meghan. There was a time when I did not know what Lannie could do.

She had put on her jacket but not mittens or hat, and the wind chewed on her exposed skin, mocking her for thinking she could come outside and live.

Meghan gathered her courage and looked straight across the street. Straight at Lannie. Firmly, without flinching, because this was not a personal thing, this was a parental order. In the game of Freeze Tag, it didn't count.

Lannie had no eyes.

Only sockets.

Meghan stopped dead, gagging, unable to walk closer.

Lannie smiled. The smile rested humanlike under the empty sockets. The smile was full of those baby teeth, small as birdseed. Meghan had a horrible feeling that birds had already been there: feeding on the face, taking the eyes, preparing to peck at the teeth.

Then Lannie was right up next to her, so wispy and unsubstantial that Meghan felt as heavy as a truck. Who had moved? How did Lannie do this —

empty herself from one spot and fill another, without Meghan ever seeing her accomplish it?

The sockets were not empty after all.

The same old eyes, bleached out and cruel, stared up at Meghan.

Lannie smirked.

It was the smirk that brought Meghan back. Such a middle-high kind of look. An *I've got what you want* taunt. Meghan's chin lifted. She would not be intimidated. "Hello, Lannie," said Meghan.

Lannie of course said nothing. Just waited.

"My father is worried," said Meghan.

Lannie of course said nothing. Just waited.

"About Jason," said Meghan.

Lannie smiled.

"He hasn't seen Jason lately," said Meghan. Talking to Lannie was like being in a track meet. She was winded from four short sentences.

"Well," said Lannie, linking her arm in Meghan's as if they were friends. "You haven't seen Jason lately either, have you?"

Lannie's arm turned to metal. It might have been a shackle on Meghan's wrist.

"It's time you saw Jason," said Lannie softly. "Come on over to my house, Meggie-Megs." Lannie had never used the nickname. It sounded somehow evil, as if Lannie had got a hold of some essential depth in Meghan and could control it.

"I just have to tell my father where he is," said Meghan, trying to resist. But Lannie did not let go. Meghan was going with Lannie Anveill whether she wanted to or not. They walked in lockstep.

I do not want to go into that house, thought Meghan Moore. I do not want to be alone with Lannie!

Lannie, who always knew what you were thinking, knew what she was thinking. "You won't be alone with me," said Lannie. Her voice dripped ugliness. Her tiny body shuddered with taunting. "Jason is there."

Lannie escorted Meghan in her front door.

It was identical to every other front door on Dark Fern Lane. It opened onto a rectangle of fake slate tiles. Four steps led down to the family room and the garage. Nine steps led up to where the kitchen opened straight onto the stairs. The living room was at the left, with only a metal railing to keep you from falling off the couch and into the stairwell. Jason had not replaced his shag carpeting. Layers of avocado green fluff, flattened in the center from years of footsteps, climbed both ways.

Lannie did not take Meghan up to the living room or kitchen.

They went down the four stairs to the fake cork floor that covered all family rooms.

Or had. Meghan's mother and father had continued the new nubbly champagne wool all the way down and across. They had replaced the plain metal railing at the living room rim with a delicate white wooden bookcase, half solid and half see through, so books were firmly placed and special possessions were beautifully displayed.

I'm thinking so hard about my own house, thought Meghan. I'm so afraid to think about Lannie's.

They did not go into Lannie's family room either.

It occurred to Meghan that she had never been in Lannie's family room. The same rather dark half-basement room with the high windows that let in so little light — the room where most people watched TV and sorted laundry and kept the video games and the board games and the outgrown Fisher-Price toys and the piles of paperbacks and magazines.

Did Lannie have any of those?

Had any family ever gathered in that family room?

When Lannie's relatives wanted to be happy, they drove away. They got in their cars.

Perhaps it was a room for solitary confinement, instead of family.

Meghan shivered.

Lannie smiled.

They turned right, into the tiny claustrophobic hall with a laundry closet on one side, a half bath on the other, and the garage door at the end. The garage door was flimsy; hollow wood that clunked lightly when closed. Most of these doors had broken and been replaced over the years. Lannie's had not.

Lannie opened it.

The two-car garage under the bedrooms was completely dark.

Lannie flipped the electric switch and the room

was flooded with light from two overhanging fluorescent tubes.

Jason sat in his Corvette.

He had a smile on his face.

One hand on the wheel.

One hand on the gearshift.

The motor was not running. But Jason was driving. The garage had been completely dark. But Jason was driving. The garage was very very cold. But Jason was driving.

Lannie's arm dropped from Meghan's.

Meghan walked slowly toward the Corvette. Jason did not look up at her. Jason did not stop smiling. Jason did not stop driving the silent motionless car.

Between the Corvette and the leaf rakes hanging against the side of the garage, Meghan stood trapped. Lannie's bright glittering eyes pierced her like stabbing icicles. Meghan backed up, pressing herself against the cold wooden studs of the garage. "You froze him."

Lannie nodded.

"But — but he's — your only family."

"No. He was just Jason."

"He didn't deserve to — umm — I mean . . ." Meghan's voice trailed off. She was having difficulty thinking. "When did you do it?" she said. "Can you undo it?"

Lannie shook her head. "It's been quite a while. I'm surprised nobody missed him before this, actually."

Meghan had been in there, in that frozen state,

where Jason was now. She well remembered the feeling. She knew every sensation Jason had had — or not had — as the cold took him over.

But she, Meghan, had returned.

How long had Jason sat behind that wheel? How long had he sat there, knowing that the glaze over his eyes was to be permanent? That the cold in his bones would be forever?

"Does West know?" whispered Meghan.

"Oh, yes." Laughter etched new lines on Lannie's parchment skin. "I made him sit next to Jason for a while," she said, smiling. "West behaves very well now."

Meghan, clutching her stomach, retreated around the Corvette.

"Don't throw up," said Lannie. "I'd only make you clean it yourself, Meghan. Jason is fine this way. It's not that much of a change from his usual personality, you know."

Lannie came closer and closer. Meghan had nowhere to go. The lawnmower blocked her exit. She had no strength in her bones anyway.

Once again Lannie's hand closed on Meghan's arm. But nothing happened. Meghan did not freeze. She did not become an ice statue. Blood still ran in her veins and thoughts still poked through her mind like electric shocks.

Oddly practical thoughts. Groceries and electric bills. How was Lannie going to keep going all winter? All year? All future years?

"I'll be fine," said Lannie. "If anybody gives me a hard time, you know what will happen to them."

Meghan knew.

"I'd prefer you didn't tell your father," said Lannie.

Meghan felt thick and hopeless.

"Because," said Lannie Anveill softly, "you know what I will do if anybody gives me a hard time, Meghan Moore."

Chapter 11

The front seat of the old truck was warm and toasty. All the short February day, sun had gleamed on yesterday's snow. The truck cab was momentarily a greenhouse in which orchids could thrive.

Meghan sat far over on her side, and West sat far over on his.

The distance between them could be measured in inches or in hearts. They did not want to touch each other. They had not discussed this. Perhaps they thought that Lannie would know. That she could read the history of this afternoon in West's eyes.

Or perhaps whatever had once been between Meghan Moore and West Trevor had grown too cold for the sun to soften.

Meghan tugged each finger of her glove forward and bent the tips down, and then tugged each finger back till it fit again. She thought deeply about the pattern knit into the gray wool. She studied the long crack in the windshield.

"There must be something!" said West. His voice was low. Lannie was a hundred miles away and yet West thought she could overhear.

I must think so, too, Meghan realized. I am afraid of what will happen tonight when she comes over here. Some afterglow of me will be lingering on West, and for Lannie it will be as vivid a message as searchlights in the dark, and she will lust to hurt one of us. That terrible desire will be back in her speech and her heart. If she has a heart.

"Some reversal!" said West urgently. "Something we can turn against her."

Oh, how I want this to end! thought Meghan. But what can be turned against a girl who possesses Lannie's power?

Yet even Lannie had to follow certain rules. Her history class had gone to the state capitol for the day and would not be back until late. Meghan constantly checked her watch and the lowering sky. What was late? How did the school define that? What if Lannie were to return when Meghan and West were sitting together?

What would she do?

Meghan was irked with herself. Meghan knew perfectly well what Lannie would do.

"Some technique," said West. And then, with a sort of ferocity in his voice, like a pit bull fastening its jaws, he spat out, "Something to *destroy* her."

Meghan swerved in the little cozy space to look at him. He was not handsome, spitting his words. He was ugly and mean. He did not see Meghan. He did not see the truck or the snow or the sky. He saw only his neighbor. Lannie Anveill. Being destroyed.

A terrible word. Armies destroy cities. People who don't want them any longer destroy dogs.

I don't want to destroy a person, thought Meghan. Even Lannie. Even with her history. I do not wish to destroy. "Can't we just cure her?" said Meghan.

"Is there a cure for evil?" demanded West.

Meghan did not know. She was new to evil.

"You're the one Lannie was going to leave frozen! She laughed when she was going to let you die in the snow! You're the one she hates most, because you have everything!" said West.

To Meghan's horrified ears, West sounded as full of hate as Lannie. As though West, too, hated Meghan, and hated the world, and all good families. His mouth looked awful. Twisted and biting down. West, her sweet good West. Meghan looked away.

"You should be first in line to wipe her out!" cried West.

But I'm not, thought Meghan. I never want to be in that line at all. I want to be in line to save people. Not the line to destroy them.

She tried to explain this to West, but he could not listen. He huffed out an angry hot lungful of air, full of swearing and cursing. In the small space between the cracked windshield and the torn seats, his words expanded. She was breathing pain and ugliness instead of oxygen.

"You think you can teach Lannie to be sweet and

forgiving?" demanded West. His anger was as frightening as Lannie's.

Meghan flinched.

"We've set an example all our lives. Both our families are kind and generous. Lannie hasn't picked up any of it, believe me. A girl who would freeze her own mother? Freeze the dog? Freeze my sister? Freeze you? Freeze Jason and keep him there like a trophy?"

I never quite believed it, thought Meghan. I was there for all of that. I was one victim, and I saw the rest. Yet even now, in the afternoon sun, I cannot quite believe it.

West changed characters as swiftly and completely as if he'd been changing clothes. He set down anger and put on contemplation. Drumming his fingers on the dashboard, West frowned in an intellectual sort of way. As if he were a professor deciding how to explain a new concept.

He was handsome again, and yet Meghan was suddenly afraid of him, too. *Too?* she thought. Am I bracketing West with Lannie? What am I afraid of?

Now she was afraid of the truck, too. The handle that did not work. The doors she could not open. The bulk of West's body that blocked the only exit. Meghan laced her ten fingers together and ordered herself to be rational.

"No," said West meditatively. "I think Lannie has to be ended."

How little emotion lay in his voice. *Lannie must be ended.*

Meghan fixed her eyes on the swirling sunlight outside the truck. The sun spoke of truth and beauty and goodness. Perhaps it was locked out. Perhaps all she needed to do was open a door.

That day Lannie froze the children.

Girls have perfect conversational recall. Boys can hardly even remember the topic. If she were to quote West to himself, West would draw a blank. I said that? he would say. No, I didn't, Meghan.

Your heart is not in this, West, Lannie had said. *I want your heart.* And West had said, *You have my heart.*

She does have his heart, thought Meghan. Horror like some grotesque virus exploded her innocence.

Lannie has his heart. That's why I don't want to touch him. She has a grip on his heart. We're alone in this truck, and yet her fingers are curled around his heart.

Even West's voice was like Lannie's. The same flatness to it, because love and heart had been ironed out of it.

No doubt Lannie had whispered that to herself when she decided she had had enough of Mrs. Anveill. *My mother must be ended.*

"West," whispered Meghan. "Did you hear yourself? Have you thought about what you're saying? *Lannie must be ended.* That's evil. It means killing Lannie."

West hardly looked at her. Now a sort of hot thick eagerness poured out of him, like a poisoned drink. "Exactly," he said.

He shared her desires, too. Her aching, throbbing desire to inflict pain.

Oh, Lannie, Lannie! thought Meghan. Give me back his heart! His fine good heart! You've taken it!

She wanted to cleanse West of Lannie. They did that in olden days. They purged people of evil. Ancient priests and ancient rituals reached down into the heart and soul and tore out the evil and left the person exhausted but clean.

West is unclean, thought Meghan. His heart is Lannie's.

"Last night," West announced casually, "I considered driving into the bridge abutment."

The bridge had been rebuilt. Huge concrete pylons and immense concrete walls.

"Lannie won't use a seatbelt," West told her. He looked happy. "I seriously thought of simply driving into the cement at seventy-five miles an hour."

"West! You'd be killed."

He nodded without regret. "Yes. We'd both be killed."

She could not bear it that West had come to this. "No, West. We will not do that. We will not think of doing that. We are not going to *end* anybody. We are not going to end Lannie and we are not going to end you."

"Then where will *this* end, Meghan?" said West. He spoke reasonably, as if discussing homework or radio stations. "Where will Lannie take us? Are we going to grow up and reach our twenties and thirties and middle age and old age, with Lannie still there threatening us? Lannie still freezing people who annoy her? Lannie still ruining all our lives?"

Meghan could not sit in the ruined truck any longer. It was too symbolic. West was the rusted-out body. "Let's go up to the house," she said. Now it was her own voice that had become toneless. All the music had passed out of her. There would be no melodies and no harmonies now. Only the flat, ironed, heartlessness of Lannie . . . and West.

West got out of the truck. Meghan slid over the seat and hit the ground with both feet. She felt better standing on the ground. A little more connected to whatever goodness was left in the world. She headed up the hill while West fussed with the truck, checking the windows and slamming the door. As if the truck mattered. As if anything mattered when a fine young man could discuss without the slightest worry the "ending" of another human being.

"I just don't see what problem you have with this, Meggie-Megs," said West, genuinely puzzled. "I mean, think of Jason in that garage! How can you possibly mind Lannie being ended when you know what she does for fun?"

"That's Lannie!" cried Meghan. "Lannie's sick and twisted. But we're not! We can't do it just because she does!"

"Now, Meggie-Megs," said West.

She could not bear it that he was abusing her baby nickname like this. Meggie-Megs had been a curly-haired toddler to whom afterschool snacks and bear hugs were the whole world. Meggie-Megs had been a name for innocence and laughter, not the "ending" of another human being.

West was still discussing Lannie's "end" as they went into the house.

His brother and sister were watching a video. Tuesday was partial to James Bond and, as Meghan entered the family room, James Bond was also facing down Evil. He would win, of course. In the movies, Good triumphed over Evil. And so cleverly. Driving the best cars and using the finest of electronic devices.

Meghan did not feel clever. She felt utterly and completed depressed, and utterly and completely unable to stop the expansion of Lannie.

"See," said West, flopping down on the big raggedy armchair, "I was also thinking that I would teach Lannie to drive. And what I could do is, send her off by herself after I've rigged whatever car I use to teach her. There'd be a nice symmetry to that besides. She killed her mother in a car. It's only fitting that she should die in a car. Don't you think so?"

Tuesday and Brown looked up from the video.

Meghan could not bear it. "West, *murder* can *not* be next on our list."

"It isn't murder," said West, slightly surprised. "It's ending Lannie."

The family room divided into two temperature zones. There was the warm and friendly side on which Tuesday and Brown sat. There was the cold and vicious side where West sat.

Meghan stood in the middle of the room, the sleet of West's plans hitting her on one side; the stunned sweetness of Tuesday and Brown warming her on the other side.

"West?" said Brown.

West did not even look at his little brother. He was caught up in a daydream, a dream in which he would do all the things to Lannie which creatures do to each other in Saturday morning cartoons: They flatten each other, they push each other off cliffs, they drop dynamite down on each other's chimneys.

Meghan knew then that she really was an ex-girlfriend.

There was no going back.

This was not West: the Trevor she loved best. This was a stranger who would slice off another life as easily as slicing a wedge off a melon.

"And then . . ." said West eagerly.

Tuesday began to cry but West did not see her. A smile was curving on West's face. Meghan could see Lannie in it, as if Lannie had taken up residence inside West.

"Or another way . . ." said West excitedly.

Brown stared at his fingernails, the way boys did, making fists and turning them up. Girls spread their fingers like fans and held them away.

Meghan went home.
She could not bear another burden.

She lay awake for a long long time. Once or twice she got out of bed and went to a window from which she could stare at Lannie's house, and think of the people who lived there: the one who breathed and the one who did not. Once or twice she got out of bed and went to a window from which she could stare at the Trevors' house, and think of the people who lived there: the friends she still understood and the friend she had lost.

And once more she got out of bed, and very, very quietly opened a door at the other end of the hall, and looked in on two sleeping parents. Truly, thought Meghan Moore, I am loved. I have seen now what it is to be unloved and I know why Lannie is jealous.

I do have everything.

In school the next day, Meghan asked Lannie to sit with her.

"What is it you want from me?" said Lannie, when they were alone together.

"I just want to talk."

Lannie shook her head. "Nobody feels that way with me. You want something from me. Say what it is." Her eyes, like faucets, ran both hot and cold. Meghan could neither look at Lannie nor look away. She could not go on being courteous and full of fibs. "I want to talk about West," she whispered. Her lips did not move easily. How did Lannie do her freezing? She had even frozen Meghan's courage, and Meghan had had so much of it when she left home this morning!

"Oh?" said Lannie.

"I'm worried about him," said Meghan.

"Oh?"

"You've made him so cold!" Meghan burst out.

Lannie smiled. "His heart is colder," she agreed.

Meghan felt herself bowing forward, the weight of her worries folding her up. Her shoulders sagged, her muscles went limp, her arms drooped.

Coldhearted.

One of those phrases people toss about easily, without consideration, without knowing what it truly means. Meghan knew. She had two cold-hearted people to go by.

And what is a cold heart?

A heart without love. Without compassion.

A heart that does not worry about others. A heart that does not care if somebody else pays a price just for being near it.

Heart and soul. They are so close! So inter-twined. What kind of soul could a coldhearted per-son have?

Perhaps, thought Meghan Moore, *no soul at all.*

Perhaps the cold heart has frozen the soul out.

"Did you touch him to do it?" she whispered.

"I didn't have to touch him. I just had to be there. Showing him my way." Lannie smiled her smile of ice and snow. "He's a good follower, West."

Meghan was crying now. Her tears were hail on her own cheeks: blisteringly cold tears that pep-pered her skin instead of running down her cheeks.

What would melt the heart of Lannie Anveill? What could possibly release the heart of West Trevor? "You froze him," said Meghan through the hail of her tears.

"Yes," said Lannie, chuckling. "He's mine."

Chapter 12

Sunshine is a blessing.

Morning is a blessing.

Agony is less and fear is diminished in the sparkle and the gold of an early sun.

Meghan was slightly restored. She dressed in a corner of her bedroom where a shaft of sunlight made a warm square on the floor. If only I could pick that up, she thought, and carry it with me. Stand in it all day long.

But she did not raise the shade to let more sun in, for Lannie's house also lay to the east.

There is a way out of this, she told herself. Then she said it out loud for additional strength. "There is a way out of this!" she called. If a cold heart has frozen West's soul, I will just have to warm him up.

She smiled to herself. "Perhaps West could be defrosted," she said to the sunshine square. It was a word for refrigerators or plastic bags of vegetables. "I am probably the only girl in America," she said ruefully, "who has to defrost her boyfriend."

Well, it made Meghan laugh, anyway. Now how

to get West to laugh so warmly? How to defrost his heart, and locate his soul, and peel him away from Lannie's influence, and save the world from Lannie?

In the sunshine, she believed that it could be done.

In the sunshine, she believed that she was the one who could do it.

And luckily, the sun stayed out all day. No clouds passed in front of it, no snowstorms blew in from Canada. Her classes in the morning were on the east side of the building and in the afternoon on the west. She never did lose that square of sunlight. And so after school, she went for help. She chose her history teacher, whom she adored and who seemed to have so many answers! The woman knew dates and wars and prime ministers and ancient enmities. She knew rivers and treaties and battles and kings.

Meghan launched right into it. "Suppose," said Meghan Moore, "that a person's soul froze. How would you teach him to love again?"

Her teacher smiled. "My dear, mankind has been trying to teach love to the frozen for thousands of years. That's half of every religion and every philosophy."

Meghan did not want to waste time reading every religion and every philosophy. "Who's right?" she said briskly.

"My dear, mankind has gone to war trying to decide who's right. They've lynched their neighbors, disowned their children, and built a million sacred edifices."

Meghan did not really want details at a time like this. "I understand, but in your opinion, who is right?"

"Everybody."

Meghan looked at her teacher with some irritation. "You wouldn't accept that answer on a quiz," she pointed out. "You'd say, 'Be more specific.' "

"Life is not a quiz," said the history teacher.

"Are you taking me seriously?" demanded Meghan. "I really need to know the answer to this question. *Who is right?*"

"And I said everybody. Love is right. In any language, in any history, in any religion, if you love your neighbor, if your heart is generous, if you show mercy and act justly, then you are right."

Love my neighbor.

Well, I have two neighbors here, thought Meghan Moore. Lannie and West.

Does this mean I have to love Lannie? That means I have to love Evil. Because Lannie is evil. She's a poison seeping from an abandoned tank into the water supply, and no one notices until all the children on the street have cancer. How can I love that?

I've always loved West. I've loved him all my life, and especially this year, and what do I have to show for it?

A cold heart in somebody else's hands.

Show mercy and act justly.

Show mercy to whom? Lannie's future victims? Lannie? Myself?

And what is justice? To do what West wants? End Lannie Anveill?

She had come for answers, and the history teacher seemed to think that they had been given to her. The history teacher smiled happily as she packed her briefcase with papers to correct that night.

To Meghan it did not feel like an answer. It felt like more questions.

She left the school. The sun still shone. The square of gold was still at her feet. But she knew nothing.

Least of all what to do next.

Chapter 13

The sun set and the snow began. Clouds as thick as continents rolled in, bleak and bruised. From out of those dark pain-ridden whirls came snow so white it stretched credulity. Nothing could be that white. That pure. That perfect.

Winter deepened in one brief afternoon.

Dark Fern Lane had never seen so much snow. It drifted thigh deep. Tires on the road surface made a whole new sound: scrunching and crunching in treads.

It was a Friday. The rules of school nights were suspended.

But not one child frolicked in the snow. Not one family had turned on a porch light or a garage light, and come out to roll a snowman in the dark. Not one snowball had been formed, not one snowfort built, not one angel made. No one had plucked the icicles from the porch overhang and pretended to be a unicorn. No one had gathered a plateful of the best and whitest snow, and poured hot maple syrup on it to make instant candy.

For another generation, yard games were over.

Those children who had been frozen like laundry — they remembered.

They had been aware, inside their motionless bodies and their unblinking eyes. They had known. They had felt Lannie's fingertips.

They were staying inside.

They would always stay inside.

Only Meghan went out into the snow, and only then because she had seen West in his mother's car stop for Lannie and drive away with her. Drive carefully, she had thought after the vanishing car. Don't do anything bad. Come home safe!

She waded through wonderful drifts, snow as deep as company on Thanksgiving.

"Meggie-Megs!" said Tuesday delightedly. "Come on in! It's freezing out there! You are so brave! Brown and I are hibernating till spring."

Meghan joined Brown and Tuesday in the family room. "Are your parents home?"

"Nope. They've taken up square dancing. Isn't that hysterical? You should see them. Dad's wearing cowboy shirts and a bowler and Mom's wearing a red calico skirt with ruffles."

Meghan wished she had seen them. It sounded so cute. She smiled, thinking of Mr. and Mrs. Trevor.

"It's good that they're gone," said Tuesday briskly. "We have things to decide."

Brown nodded. He sat up on the edge of the couch. Whatever they were going to decide could not be done slouching. "First," said Brown, "how much does West actually like her?"

Here we go again, thought Meghan. There's no getting away from Lannie Anveill.

"When West kisses Lannie, it looks real," said Brown. "Is he an actor? Or does he love her?"

"He started as an actor," said Tuesday, "but I think it became real. That's a danger with playing games so hard and so well. You forget it's a game. It gets into your bloodstream." Tuesday stood up. "Microwave popcorn anybody? Cheese or plain buttered?"

"Plain buttered," said Brown. "It's not only a game, but Lannie has beaten him at it. He's getting to be as sick and twisted as she is."

Tuesday brought out the popcorn. Their six hands went into the bowl together. They sat close to share. Food helps a person think.

"I have to believe," said Meghan, munching, "that good is stronger than evil. That somehow this will work out all right."

"It won't," said Tuesday.

"I saw Jason," said Brown. He crammed more popcorn into his mouth.

"Well, there's no helping him now," said Tuesday. "And probably no helping West either. We have to look out for ourselves."

The popcorn stuck in Meghan's throat.

"So the question here is," said Brown, rubbing a popcorn against the side of the bowl to slick up extra butter and salt, "how do we end Lannie?"

The cold seeped into Meghan's heart again. Yet another sweet Trevor suggesting that Lannie should be "ended."

"Could she freeze herself?" asked Tuesday. "Could we play Freeze Tag and somehow she freezes herself?"

Brown shook his head. "If that could happen, she'd have frozen herself when she brushed her hair or put on lipstick."

"I'm thirsty," said Tuesday. "Meggie-Megs, you want Coke, Dr. Pepper, cider, hot chocolate, raspberry ginger ale, or milk?"

This was too big a decision to be executed from the family room. The three of them went into the kitchen to inspect the actual containers. Once she had seen the bottles, Meghan knew she needed water first, to wash down the salt and butter, and then she could concentrate on the hot chocolate. "Do you have marshmallows?" she said.

"It comes with them. See?"

Meghan saw. She would ask her mother to get that kind. "I could offer myself," said Meghan. "I could say: Here. Freeze me. I am yours. Do not hurt other people who are not involved."

"Lannie'd just freeze you and leave you," said Brown, "and go on to her next victim. You wouldn't accomplish anything by that except to join Jennifer or Jacqueline or whoever she is on the hospital ward."

"I thought Lannie unfroze her."

"That was a while ago. There's been another one."

"What did Jennifer or Jacqueline do to Lannie?"

"Wasn't friendly, I guess."

"I know," said Tuesday. "We could lock her away."

"You own a jail, maybe?" said Brown. He shrugged and gave up. He found the remote and turned on the television. This was Brown's only answer to all difficulties.

Homework too hard? Watch TV.

Family too annoying? Watch TV.

Lannie too scary? Watch TV.

It had very little to do with the history teacher's answer to all difficulties. Mercy and justice.

Tuesday and Meghan watched helplessly. It's difficult to have a television on and not get sucked in. How remote, how impossible the family on the TV screen seemed. How could they laugh so hard and so often?

We used to laugh like that, thought Meghan. Back before we knew all about Lannie Anveill.

Beneath her feet she felt the rising and slamming of the automatic garage door, rarely used. She heard the growl of a car engine and its abrupt cessation. She heard a door slam. West is here, she thought.

She heard a second door slam.

"Lannie's with him," said Tuesday.

Brown turned up the television volume. It might have been a weapon or camoflauge. He was wrapped in a canned laugh track, safe even from Lannie Anveill.

Feet hit the stairs, and up through the raised ranch came West and Lannie.

Meghan's grandmother had had an awful saying of which she was very fond: Speak of the devil, and he appears.

They had spoken of Lannie, and she had appeared.

No one said hello.

Brown did not look up from the television. Tuesday did not look up from the popcorn. West did not look up from his shoes. Meghan practiced locking her fingers together.

Lannie chuckled.

It was such an inappropriate sound that Meghan did look up. She caught Lannie unaware. Lannie was nervous.

Because we don't like her! thought Meghan, astonished to see this flicker of humanness. Lannie wants to be popular like anybody else. We're afraid of her and we don't want her around and it makes her nervous!

Lannie and West dropped onto the couch opposite Meghan and Tuesday. It's good they have two sofas, thought Meghan. It would be tricky to have to sit next to each other.

"Turn that down," said Lannie.

Brown did not pretend he couldn't hear her. He notched the volume down, and he didn't play around, taking it slowly and being infuriating. He didn't want to see that finger of hers moving toward him.

The people on television giggled and sparred and chatted but you could not quite hear them; they might suddenly have become ghosts whose presence was only fractional.

Lannie smiled.

West looked away.

"Popcorn?" said Tuesday brightly.

"We ate," said West.

So they sat, waiting for Lannie to leave, waiting for the torture to be over. But this was Lannie, of course, who enjoyed torture, and so she was not going to leave.

"Oh!" said Brown suddenly.

They all looked at him.

He sparkled, the way you do when you've just had a brilliant idea. "Lannie!" said Brown.

She raised her eyebrows.

"I know what! Why don't you and I go out?" he said. "I'd be a great date. And that way, Meghan could still be with West."

Meghan was so touched she wanted to weep. Brown was offering himself in exchange.

Lannie hooted with laughter. "You?" she said. "You're a little boy! You're eleven years old! Get a life! You're so pathetic, Brown."

"You're the one who's pathetic! You know perfectly well, nobody would ever date you because he wanted to!" shouted Brown. "You have to threaten them with freezing to get them to sit in the same room with you. You have to keep Jason in the car to scare everybody to death just in order to get a ride to school!"

"West promised to like me best," said Lannie defensively, "and he does. So there."

"He does not!" screamed Tuesday. "He hates you! He loves Meghan!"

I cannot bear it, thought Meghan. I cannot go on like this. I will have to give up. I will have to have another life, with other friends.

Meghan looked at the three Trevors as if for the last time. She thought of school and all the people she knew there — thought of scrounging among them like a bag lady, hoping to find a discarded friend for herself. She thought: I'm a sophomore and I have nobody. I have to start all over.

"Do you really love Meghan?" Lannie asked West in a deathly cold voice. She held her hands away from her sides, like a police officer whose holster and stick make him walk funny. But Lannie didn't need a holster nor a stick. Just a fingertip.

"Of course not," said West. He put his arms around Lannie. She vanished in his embrace, as small as a kindergartner. Then he kissed her hair.

"How romantic," said Brown. "Must be like kissing a bale of hay."

West did not respond to this. Nor did he even glance at Meghan, whose hair he had once loved to touch. Is he protecting me? wondered Meghan. Or has he forgotten me? I can't tell. I don't know.

"Go home and get warmer clothes, Lannie," said West. "We'll go ice skating. It's Friday. The rink's open till midnight."

Lannie said shyly, flirtatiously, "I'm not very good."

West smiled. "I'll hold you up."

Meghan's heart broke.

Did anybody ever want to hear anything else? *I'll hold you up.* It's what we all want, thought Meghan. Somebody to catch us when we're afraid of falling.

Oh how I want him back! I want West Trevor! We held *each other* up. We were a pair. A perfect pair.

Meghan was weary. I'm going home, she thought. There's no point in coming back here. I have to stay away and start over. By myself.

Silently and seemingly without motion, Lannie eased herself out of the Trevor house. Lannie's vanishing always gave Meghan the shivers.

From across the room West said, "Never touch me again, Meghan."

She thought she would fall over. He didn't have to say that! He could leave it alone, without stabbing her with those words!

"Lannie knows we're meeting," West said tonelessly. "She gave me her power. If I touch anybody other than Lannie, they'll freeze."

West left to get the car out again, get Lannie again, go hopelessly on with his half-life again.

Brown watched his brother leave.

Tuesday watched her brother leave.

But Meghan could not bear to look at the West she would never again have, and so she watched Tuesday.

A strange flicker crossed her best friend's face.

An expression both calculating and cruel.

Meghan had to look away, and when she looked back, the expression was gone, and Meghan convinced herself she had never seen it. Tuesday — sweet Tuesday of summer nights and pink lemonade — would not look like that.

It was the face of a cold heart.

A frozen soul.

Chapter 14

Snow fell for days.

They had never experienced such weather. The sky would not change, would not back off, would not turn clear and blue. Endlessly, the sky dumped snow down upon them. School was canceled because the snowplows could not keep up with the amazing amounts of snow. After a while there was no place for the plows to push the snow, and the roads became narrower, flanked by mountain ranges of previously shoveled snow.

Brown didn't mind. He was the kind of person who could watch a million hours of television and then watch a million more. He just sat there with the TV on, staring. Tuesday had a "kitchen attack" and suddenly made real sugar cookies which she cut out in hearts and decorated with red glaze or chocolate chips.

Tuesday called Meghan to see if she had any other cookie cutters because Tuesday had a lot more cookie dough and no more shapes.

Meghan's mother had once been given a collection

of cookie cutters. They were still in the original box, lying on the original white tissue.

So much for finding new friends, thought Meghan. She put on her layers of protection against the winter and stormed her way to the Trevors' with her collection. She and Tuesday rolled out dough on the kitchen counter and argued whether — in February — they could properly use the Christmas tree or the Santa.

There was a knock at the front door.

Tuesday went to get it. Meghan took the opportunity to snitch a long thin slice of raw dough. Meghan loved raw cookie dough.

"Hi," said Lannie at the door. Like a normal person. A regular greeting and everything.

Meghan pressed herself into the corner of the kitchen, where she would be invisible if Lannie came up the stairs.

"Hi, Lannie," said Tuesday.

"Is West here?"

"Not yet. He went out to get a part for his truck. He's going to work on it today."

West hasn't looked at his truck in ages, thought Meghan. Strange how a person's only sister sees so little. You would think Tuesday would know that West is so caught between Lannie and real life that rusted trucks and stalled engines have slipped his mind. But no, she thinks he's still down there every day, working on the Chevy.

"Why don't you wait for West in the truck?" said Tuesday.

It's awfully cold out, thought Meghan. I'm not

sure that Lannie should be . . . what am I doing?

Meghan shook off her thoughts.

I'm trying to protect Lannie's health? I don't mind if Lannie catches cold. I hope Lannie gets such a bad cold she's home for a year!

"West will be back in a while and you know the first thing he'll do is run down there to look at his truck," said Tuesday.

From her corner Meghan looked out the kitchen window. There was only one, and it was a small dark square above the sink. Mrs. Trevor was trying to grow little plants on that window, but they didn't get enough sun, and all she had were thin bottles of water and sad little cuttings of fading greens. There had been no sunset because the sun had never been visible. The dark sky had simply grown darker, and now, in the hour before supper, the darkness had a fullness to it, as if it had finally consumed everything in its path and was ready for a nap.

Tuesday went on and on about the truck.

After a while, Brown woke from his television coma and joined Tuesday in the little entry between the stairs. "Here," he said, "I'll put on the backyard light for you." He hit the switch that turned on the light at the bottom of the deck stairs which led up to the kitchen door. Now the snow sparkled.

Barely, way down the sloping yard, Meghan could see the mounded tops of a row of cedars that had grown up near the truck. You could not quite see down as low as the truck. The white spires of the cedars marked the spot.

How peacefully the snow lay. Snow covers all ugliness, thought Meghan.

Tuesday coaxed Lannie around the house. Tuesday even went with her partway, although Tuesday had neither coat nor boots on. "He'll be there soon," Tuesday said twice.

Lannie waded down the sloping yard, past the snow covered vines and hedges and underbrush. Meghan turned off the kitchen lights so that Lannie would not see her, illuminated next to the cookie dough. She could hardly see Lannie. In fact, Lannie's shadow was clearer than the real Lannie.

Lannie's little body, forcing itself against the high drifts and packed snow, dipped down and disappeared from sight.

Meghan pulled the shade over the kitchen window before she turned the light back on.

"Now let's set the table," said Tuesday briskly. "Mom's exhausted from her new job. I've promised to do dinner twice a week. She cut a seafood recipe out of *Family Circle*. Doesn't this look yummy? You chop the onions and sauté them, and I'll start the biscuits."

"What does sauté mean?" said Meghan uneasily. She was not familiar with kitchens. Her own family had take-out, or fixed meals that involved heating rather than recipes, like steak and baked potatoes.

In the end, Tuesday even had to demonstrate the purpose of the chopping board. Had to show Meghan how to dice the onion without also dicing her fingertips. How to scrape the onions into the skillet without dumping half of them in the crack between the stove and the counter. "This is work," said Meghan. "I'm exhausted from a single onion."

She and Tuesday giggled.

"Now you've got to prepare the scallops," said Tuesday. She took a wrapped package out of the meat compartment of the refrigerator and ripped it open.

"Those horrible mushy white things? We're going to eat those?" Meghan was horrified.

"Yes. We're going to love them. Now here's what you do."

And then she had to do things with garlic as well, and parsley had to be torn, and then she was given a tiny little broom, or paintbrush, with which to slather melted butter on the tops of the almost-baked biscuits. When they came out of the oven again, minutes later, they were crusty and golden and smelled of heaven.

There was quite a rush as everybody else got home, and the table had to be set, and her parents had to be telephoned for permission for Meghan to eat at the Trevors' again, and Meghan had to work through her guilt for once again not being home with her own family.

The real treat was sitting next to West again.

His smile was normal, his laugh was genuine.

Mr. Trevor had had a great day at work and regaled them with stories. "This is the best dinner I've had in years!" he kept saying. "Meghan, you did the garlic and onion?"

"I taught her how, Dad," said Tuesday.

He shook his head proudly. "What a pair!"

"I'll have seconds," said West.

Meghan was beaming.

"Excellent dinner," pronounced Mrs. Trevor. Then she giggled in that special Trevor way. "Of course, I'd like any meal that somebody else fixed, so my standards are pretty low."

"You guys would not believe," said Tuesday, "what I had to teach old Meggie-Megs here. Good grief. She doesn't know an onion from a potato."

"What's for dessert?" said Mr. Trevor, holding a fork in one hand and a spoon in the other, ready for any eating style.

"Drop that silver," said Meghan.

"Cookies," said Tuesday, bringing out a tray lined with a Christmas napkin she'd dug up from somewhere.

"Santa Clauses!" shouted Mr. Trevor. He bit off a Santa head and declared it the tastiest cookie he'd had in his life.

Meghan had never dreamed that the mere cooking of food could bring so many compliments. She would have to tell her parents. Perhaps the Moores would try cooking, too, one day.

West cleared the table, scraped the dishes, loaded the dishwasher, ran hot soapy water for the pots. Dishes had always been his job. And he had never complained. His mother put on the coffee. Mr. and Mrs. Trevor always liked to sit around the table sipping that awful stuff after a big meal.

"So," said Mrs. Trevor, smiling broadly at her

son, and then equally broadly at Meghan, "you two are back together again? Lannie's out of the picture?"

I forgot Lannie! She's still waiting for him down in the truck! Meghan swerved to look at Tuesday, so Tuesday would give West the message. Certainly Meghan didn't want to deliver it. She was as full of happiness as the night was full of dark. She didn't even want to utter the name, because it would break her happy spell like an icicle hitting the pavement.

Both Tuesday's eyelids went down slowly, in a sort of double wink. How like Lannie she suddenly looked. Hooded, evil eyes. Eyes that had seen terrible things. Eyes that had seen through to the other side.

"Lannie's out of the picture," agreed Tuesday. She, too, smiled broadly. She met West's eyes and now his smile came out. Meghan could not move. Out of the corner of her eyes she checked Brown. No smile had ever been wider.

Meghan did not need to be out in the snow to be cold. Her hands, her heart, her thoughts: They chilled as if her friends had refrigerated her.

"All we need now," said Mr. Trevor, "is ice cream. A really good dinner isn't done till you've had your ice cream. Meghan, dish it out!"

Meghan got up from the table. She circled the big flat dining room table, and crossed the kitchen to the refrigerator.

The inside of the freezer was rimmed with frost crystals. Ice cubes tumbled out of the ice maker and fell into a clear plastic box. They looked like stones for a pyramid. Her fingers grazed the metal edge of the freezer and for a scary moment they stuck to the cold. She peeled herself away and got the ice cream container out.

So cold in there. How chilly the boxes of vegetables and desserts must be. Meghan shut the door, leaving the cold boxes to their dark frozen lives. They had to lie there until somebody wanted them. They had no exit without human hands. There were no handles on the insides of refrigerator doors.

Handles.

There are no handles on the inside of the truck doors, either, thought Meghan Moore. Lannie cannot get out of the truck.

Nobody knows she's there.

The snow is coming down. The truck is getting colder and colder. Lannie can scream and kick and bite. But she will never get out. There are no handles on the inside.

By morning . . .

By morning, Lannie Anveill will be frozen.

Like Jason, she will sit behind the wheel. She may sit all winter. Because Mr. and Mrs. Trevor never go down there.

And nobody else knows she's there.

"I boiled water," said Mrs. Trevor cheerily. "People who don't want coffee with their ice cream may have tea, herb tea, spiced cider, or instant hot chocolate."

West smiled. He would have coffee, please. Cream and sugar.

Tuesday smiled. She would have herb tea, please. With honey.

Brown smiled. He would have hot chocolate, please.

They were not smiling for coffee, tea, or chocolate.

They were smiling because they knew where Lannie was.

Those were not even smiles across their faces.

They were gashes.

Tuesday knew.

West knew.

And Brown, grinning down into his ice cream — Brown knew.

"Meghan?" said Mrs. Trevor.

"Spiced cider," said Meghan. It's not my responsibility, she thought. Tuesday sent her down there. Tuesday's the one letting it happen.

Only three people would know where Lannie Anveill was. How she got there. What happened to her.

No.

Actually, four people.

Three Trevors . . . *and one Moore.*

Meghan Moore.

Meghan's cider spilled on the table.

She set the mug down. Then set her trembling hand on her lap.

No. West. We will not do that. We will not even think of doing that.

Then where will this end, Meghan? Where will Lannie take us? Are we going to grow up and reach our twenties and thirties and middle age and old page, with Lannie still there threatening us, ruining our lives?

You won, Lannie. You froze him.

Yes. He's mine.

Evil can infect. Evil can spread. Evil has such great and terrible power that it infiltrates even the best of human beings.

I, thought Meghan Moore, am the one who became evil.

I am the one sitting here with a mug of spiced cider, waiting for the cold and terrible hours of night to pass, so that Lannie Anveill turns to ice and snow.

My heart.

My heart is frozen.

Meghan Moore got up from the table. She walked to the back door. It was difficult. Her feet dragged and she bumped into the jamb. The doorknob did not fit her hand and the wind when she opened the door assaulted her.

She heard voices behind her, but they were Trevor voices. The voices of people to whom things came easily. The voices of people who expected things to work out their way. Meghan did not know if she still loved the Trevors.

The one I have to love most, she thought, is me.

If I don't love myself, I cannot go on.

The cold was no longer an enemy. Instead it woke her and embraced her with its demands.

This is what it means, thought Meghan Moore, to choose the lesser of two evils. Lannie is evil, but it would be more evil to stand aside and silently let her die.

Meghan had never gone through snow so deep, through darkness so thick. She found the truck by feel. She opened the door of the cab and Lannie fell into her arms.

Meghan helped Lannie walk.

"Come in my house where it's warm," said Meghan.

Lannie said nothing.

Perhaps she was too cold to speak.

Or perhaps . . . she had waited all her life to come in where it was warm.

CAROLINE B. COONEY lives in a small seacoast village in Connecticut. She writes every day and then takes a long walk on the beach to figure out what she's going to write the following day. She's written more than seventy books for young people, including *The Party's Over*; the acclaimed *The Face on the Milk Carton* quartet; *Flight 116 Is Down*, which won the 1994 Golden Sower Award for Young Adults and the 1995 Rebecca Caudill Young Readers' Book Award, and was selected as an ALA Recommended Book for the Reluctant Young Adult Reader; *Flash Fire*; *Emergency Room*; *The Stranger*; *Twins*; *Mummy*; and *Fatality*. *Wanted!* and *The Terrorist* were both 1998 ALA Quick Picks for Reluctant Young Adult Readers.

Ms. Cooney reads as much as possible and has three grown children and two granddaughters.